Pamela Prendergast and the Fatal Accident

Cecilia Peartree

KDP print edition
Cover design Canva (cover image Sheila Perry)

CONTENTS

Chapter 1 Moving Day

The door-bell rang just as Pamela was sealing up the next box. The tape tangled in her fingers when she looked up from her task, irritated by the interruption. It was much too early for the removal men. They were booked for late morning, and they didn't have far to go, so they shouldn't have bothered trying to make an early start.

She set the roll of tape aside and walked out of the kitchen and down the hall to the front door. The bell rang again before she got there, which didn't improve her mood.

'All right, all right,' she mumbled. 'I'm on my way.'

She flung the door open wide, prepared to get very cross with whoever was outside.

A teenage boy stood there, a large cardboard box in his arms. He thrust the box towards her.

'Mrs Prendergast?' he said.

'What's this?'

She refused to take the box. She had more than enough boxes to deal with today without accepting an extra one from a perfect stranger.

Or was he a stranger? There was something oddly familiar about him, although she didn't see how there could be, for she didn't know any teenage boys. It was something about his eyes, dark and deep-set, and glaring at her in a way that didn't make sense.

'I can't keep them any longer,' he said, and pushed the box at her.

She had to take it, because she could see he was going to let go anyway, and she didn't know anything about the contents. They could be breakable, for all she knew, and the last thing she needed at this point was to have to sweep up broken glass or crockery from the small courtyard outside her door.

As soon as he saw that she had a firm grasp on the cardboard, he turned on his heel and went off up the steps to street level without another word.

'No, wait!'

Something moved inside the box, and she adjusted her grip accordingly. She'd have to put it down somewhere safe before following the boy. Was it even worth trying to catch him? At least she could try and see which way he went, not that she would learn much from that. He might easily just be planning to jump on the next bus and go almost anywhere.

She felt movement under her fingers again, almost as if something might be wriggling. Dear God, was there something alive inside?

Pamela turned decisively and went back into the flat. She carried the box into the kitchen, closing the door behind her, and put it down on the floor not far from the back door. At least then she'd be able to use the kitchen brush to sweep whatever it was out to the communal garden if it turned out to be…

There was a muffled yap from inside the container.

She took a step back, and then a step forwards. She bent and ripped the tape off the top of the box and folded back the flaps. And met the blank stares of two small dogs. She was sure her own expression would have seemed just as blank if she'd happened to see it in a mirror at that moment.

One of the dogs, presumably the bolder one, pushed its way past the other one and scrambled up out of the box. It was a small terrier – probably a Yorkie, in which case, she thought it could do with having its straggly fringe brushed out and maybe trimmed a little. It sniffed around her feet for a moment and then sat down on them with a heavy sigh.

Pamela reached a tentative hand down towards the other dog, which gave her a quick lick before scrambling out of the box to join its companion.

'What am I supposed to do with you two?' she murmured.

She got down on her hands and knees to look at them more closely and to pet them a little. One had on a blue collar and the other a pink one, and as she looked in vain for a tag with a useful name, address or phone number on it, she found a tightly rolled piece of paper tucked into the pink collar.

To avoid having to look at the paper or to think about what to do with the dogs, she took them out to the garden for a few minutes. The timid one with the pink collar hid behind her legs and shivered, while the other dog was brave until he heard a noise from one of the upstairs flats, when he raced back indoors. Back in the kitchen she located an odd saucer and put some water in it for them, then made herself a coffee and found the biscuit tin.

Pamela had got through three of the shortbread biscuits she'd deliberately saved to eat after the move, when she had thought she might need cheering up, before she could bring herself to unroll the piece of paper and read the contents.

If she had expected some kind of explanation about why the dogs were here, she would have been disappointed. Still, at least there were the names of the dogs, and some minimalist feeding instructions, and an assurance that all their vaccinations were up-to-date. All the information was neatly printed. Tiger and Lily. Hmm. Who called a dog Tiger? It did seem incongruous in the extreme.

She turned the page over. There was something scrawled on the back.

'I know you'll look after them.'

Hmph. Well, that was more than she knew herself. How could some strange teenage boy know that? It had been incredibly irresponsible of him to leave them with her.

On the other hand, she mused as she glanced down at her feet, where the two dogs nestled, maybe she needed them as much as they needed her. She should probably take them straight to the cat and dog home or even to the police before she became attached to them, but if she did that she would probably never know what happened to them next, and there would be nothing connecting her to the teenage boy with the eerily familiar eyes.

A few hours later, some time in the afternoon, Pamela wandered through the flat for the last time. It was empty now, of course – no longer the home she and Paul had lived more or less happily in, but a blank canvas waiting for a new artist to paint something different on. But fortunately she didn't have much time to spend on idle reflection. The removal men had been and gone, and would be expecting her at the bungalow as soon as they'd had their lunch break. The kettle and coffee mugs and biscuit tin were in the car, as were the two little terriers. For the short journey she had put them back in the box they'd arrived in, only this time she'd made holes in the side for them to look out of and added an old jumper in for them to lie on.

She locked the front door for the last time, went up the steps and handed over the keys to the man waiting at the top. She didn't look back at the courtyard. Like the flat, it was no longer hers. The wooden bench and the containers with little evergreen bushes in them had all gone away with the removal men. She could arrange them outside her new front door according to her own wishes, maybe interspersing the formal evergreens with pots of geraniums or petunias. Paul hadn't thought flowers were appropriate for the stark New Town courtyard. It wasn't up to Paul any longer.

Tiger and Lily were annoying enough during the car journey to take her mind off everything else. They yapped frantically every time the car stopped, and the bold one, whom she had decided must be male, got his paw stuck in one of the peepholes she'd made in the box and she had to stop in a loading bay somewhere to get him free. The relatively short distance from the New Town to Cramond seemed almost endless, and for once it wasn't the fault of the traffic or the roadworks.

'I didn't know you had a dog,' remarked one of the removal men as she opened the car door in her new driveway.

She rolled her eyes. 'Neither did I, until very recently.'

'Still, it's a grand place for walks around here,' he said. 'The beach, and the river, and the island, if the tides are right.'

Pamela suppressed a shudder. Cramond Island. She had told herself it didn't matter, that she wouldn't have to go there or even see the place. It wasn't visible from the windows of the bungalow – she had checked up on that, at least. But now that she had the dogs, she supposed she'd have to take them for walks somewhere or other. Not to the island, though. Never there.

By the end of the afternoon, it was all done. The furniture at least had been distributed to the correct rooms, even if there were still most of the boxes to unpack. She might start with the books. Though she really should sort out her studio so that she could get back to work. Her latest illustration project wouldn't finish itself, after all.

Dog food.

She would have to go out for dog food. The terriers had sprung to life again after their travel ordeal, such as it was, and were looking at her expectantly. Or maybe that was just her imagination.

Was it safe to leave them in the bungalow while she went out foraging? She didn't think she could face the task of wrestling them back into the box. And after all, she hadn't unpacked much so surely there wasn't much mischief for them to get up to.

Half an hour later Pamela, laden with dog food, opened her new front door to be greeted by the two small terriers flinging themselves at her legs and almost knocking her over. They started yapping and bouncing around in the restricted space, and all she could do was to stand still until they paused for breath.

Tiger and Lily hadn't done a lot of damage while she was out. There were tooth-marks in the top of one of the kitchen boxes, but they hadn't had time to make much impact, and the contents were still intact. They gobbled up the dog food almost as soon as it landed in the saucers she'd put down for them, and then fell asleep in a heap on the back doormat.

It wasn't quite the moving day she had planned, but at least she had got here.

Chapter 2 Promenade

Pamela hadn't even considered the concept of dog-proofing her new garden until the moment she opened the back door to let the two little terriers run free in the early morning sunshine. Lily, identifiable by her pink collar, hung back, evidently waiting for some kind of reassurance that Pamela hadn't known she was supposed to give, but Tiger made straight for the gap in the fence where one of the wooden slats had fallen over sideways, wriggled through and vanished from sight.

Pamela groaned and ventured into the garden to investigate.

'Tiger!' she hissed, hoping he would come back before the next-door neighbour noticed him. 'Come and get your breakfast,' she added, although she had no idea whether the animal's vocabulary stretched to the word 'breakfast' or not.

Lily gave a helpful yap.

There was an answering yap from the garden beyond the fence, and Tiger bounded back through. Sibling affection, presumably. Pamela hurried over to the fallen fence slat and tried to wedge it across the gap. Maybe if she padded it out with handfuls of weeds round the sides…

She realised, glancing around her, that the garden, although quite picturesque, wasn't quite as well-kept as she and Paul had fondly imagined it to be, that first time they'd come to look at the place. She had a horrible feeling the house might turn out to be in a similar state, although admittedly it was hard to tell at the moment, with every available surface cluttered with cardboard boxes.

She and Lily walked the perimeter of the garden for a few moments while Tiger poked about near the fence, presumably hoping to find another escape route. Pamela kept an eye on him and thought she was ready to spring into action if he did. And there he went again! This time she was able to make a grab for him before he vanished. She clasped him firmly round the stomach and dragged him back on to her own property.

'See?' she said to him sternly. 'You have to get up pretty early in the morning to catch me out.'

He stared at her blankly again. She inspected the latest gap in the fence, and this time she was able to push the loose slat firmly into place. How long it would stay like that was anybody's guess. She'd better get somebody to have a good look at all the fences before some disaster struck. Quite apart from annoying the neighbours, Tiger could escape on to the road and have an accident.

She hurried them both back into the house before anything worse happened. They might settle down for a while if she made a cosy bed for them in the corner of her favourite chair, and then she could get on with creating a studio from the room at the back of the house that must have been meant to be a spare bedroom. Or maybe a nursery. The walls had been painted a pale primrose yellow, though she intended eventually to give them a coat of plain white. At least there weren't any bunnies or teddies to be seen.

A couple of hours later she had the room in a functional state, although she still had an odd reluctance to settle down to work there. The computer and her most urgent project files had travelled to Cramond with her in the car, so everything was to hand. There was no excuse not to get on with it.

Except...

She was still contemplating the sight of the tidy desk and the unopened laptop when there was a flurry of yapping from the front room.

She got down the hall in time to save the envelope that had just come through the letterbox from the jaws of doom. Or Tiger's mouth, depending on how you looked at it. That would be something to watch out for in future.

The envelope was from her lawyers. She had noticed while contemplating her work-station that sunshine was streaming into the room, so it was definitely too lovely a day to read through screeds of legal language. Far better to use the weather as an excuse to walk the dogs. After all, tomorrow could be cold and wet. This afternoon could be cold and wet, for that matter. It might even snow, although she supposed that was unlikely by the end of April.

Pamela fetched the dogs' leads, and snatched up the car keys when she saw them on the hall shelf. She wouldn't walk down towards the mouth of the River Almond, which would have been the easiest option, and probably the most scenic too. If she did that, she would see the causeway to the island at close quarters, and she wasn't ready for that just yet. Instead she would drive round to Silverknowes and walk the dogs along the promenade from there. She knew there was plenty of parking and space for walking. It might be less busy there too than at the picturesque Cramond harbour. She might not even have to speak to anybody, whereas if she set off on foot she'd have to pass some of the neighbouring houses and she would be a sitting duck for gossipy strangers with too much time on their hands.

The plan was effective up to a point.

She had decided to keep the dogs on their leads for this first walk. She had no idea whether they would come back to her if she let them go. To judge by Tiger's reaction to being loose in the garden, they probably wouldn't. She would build up gradually to letting them run free.

Despite everything, she enjoyed the walk at first. The promenade ran along the shore of the Firth of Forth, so there was a large expanse of water just over the sea wall. She could see a couple of large boats in the middle distance – one of them might be a cruise ship – and every so often a plane would fly almost overhead, descending towards the airport.

It all started to go wrong when a strange dog ran up to the two little terriers. It wasn't that much bigger than them, and it seemed to want to play and not to fight, but Lily immediately tried to hide behind Pamela, causing the leads to tangle, and Tiger took exception to that and yapped, and the other dog seemed to take this as a sign of hostility and bared its teeth at him, at which he lunged forward, jerking Pamela with him.

For a horrible moment she thought she was about to fall on top of at least one of the dogs, but somebody grabbed her by the arm at the last moment and hauled her upright.

'Are you all right?' enquired an anxious voice, almost in her ear.

'I'm fine, thanks.'

'I thought you were going to squash this wee one flat,' said the voice.

Something pushed against her legs and she saw Lily gazing up at her, looking even more terrified than before.

Pamela turned towards her rescuer.

'I'm sorry about my Darren,' said the woman, indicating the slightly larger dog with a sweep of her hand. 'He doesn't mean any harm but he's a bit pushy.'

Darren seemed an odd name for a dog, but then Tiger and Lily certainly weren't any better. At least the woman had dragged him away and was holding him firmly by the collar, so that he wasn't standing over Tiger any longer. Darren was a thin dog who trembled in his owner's grasp.

'That's all right,' said Pamela. 'These two are new here.'

The woman stared at them, apparently bewildered. 'You live somewhere about, do you?'

Pamela shook her head. 'Not really. I've got the car up there at the top.'

'Mmhm,' said the woman. 'Have you had the two of them long?'

Was there an accusing note in her voice now? Did she think Pamela had stolen the dogs? Any moment now, the woman would be asking where she'd got them. And to be fair, Pamela's account of how the two terriers had come into her possession would sound quite suspicious. Maybe she should have taken them to the police or the cat and dog home after all. Although when she looked down at Lily's big beseeching eyes, she knew she wouldn't be able to bring herself to abandon the dog to strangers. How could the boy have done it?

'Not very long,' she said. She took out her phone and pretended to check the time. 'I'd better be getting back now.'

She picked up Lily and tugged at Tiger's lead.

She could almost feel the woman watching her as she hurried back along the promenade and up the slope to where her car was parked. She didn't look back, but as she drove away from the parking space she could see the woman still staring in her direction from somewhere near the café down below. She wouldn't be able to see the car number-plate from there, surely?

There was no reason for her to feel guilty, or obscurely anxious. The boy had asked her – begged her – to look after the dogs. He had known her name. He wasn't a random stranger, and there must have been some reason for him to come to her door.

As Pamela drove back to the bungalow by the unnecessarily circuitous route that had been decreed by the city council, her feeling of guilt diminished a little, although it was swiftly replaced by a more general unease. Should she have demanded more information from the boy? And where had she seen him before?

Once they were back at the bungalow – home - she re-filled the dogs' water dish, hurried through to her new studio and sketched a quick portrait of what she remembered of the boy. It still didn't ring any bells. She set it aside to look at again later.

Chapter 3 Neighbours

After lunch, Pamela opened the back door and took the lawyer's letter out to the bench, which the removal men had placed against the wall of the bungalow. That position would do for now, but she could see it would soon be in the shade. Maybe a paved area down at the end of the garden and some new garden furniture? Even a summer-house? She felt the faint stirrings of enthusiasm for her new home. She couldn't have had a summer-house in the New Town. Apart from the fact that only the small courtyard outside her front door had actually belonged to her, she was sure somebody would have objected to any garden structure that they thought was out of keeping with the hallowed architecture.

The two little terriers lay down in the long grass – she didn't have a mower. That was another thing she'd never needed before. Maybe they would go back to sleep for a while.

She had just turned over the first page of the letter, having failed to understand much of the content so far, when the yapping sound reached her ears. She glanced up. There was no sign of either of the dogs. Lily might have run into the house, of course, but surely Tiger...

She had risen to her feet, trying to work out what direction the yapping was coming from, when a large man suddenly appeared round the corner of the bungalow. There was a side gate, of course. She'd forgotten about that. Was there any way of fitting a proper lock to it? A padlock? Surely she could do something like that herself.

All these thoughts flew through her mind as she stared at the man, finally noticing he had a small dog in his arms. Tiger, who fortunately wasn't living up to the ferocity of his name.

'Tiger,' she said, feeling even more irritated by the stupid names.

Lily appeared at the back door at that moment.

The man smiled. 'He does seem to see the world as his jungle, you're right.'

'No, I didn't mean… His name's Tiger, I'm afraid.'

'You'd better get somebody to look at that side gate of yours,' he said. 'The gatepost's rotten. The whole thing's going to collapse one of those days.'

He handed the dog over to her. She clutched at the animal, suddenly wary. She'd seen this man before.

'Mrs Prendergast,' he said. He had stopped smiling now. 'We seem to be neighbours.'

He sounded as if he was exasperated by the fact.

'I've only just moved in,' she said. 'Yesterday.'

If she had known Detective Chief Inspector Mitchell lived in the next bungalow along, she would have thought twice about buying this house, contracts or no contracts. She suspected her lawyer would have had something to say about that, though.

She glanced back at the letter she'd been reading. One of the pages had come loose and was blowing away down the garden.

'I'll just get that,' she said.

'No, allow me,' he said. 'You seem to have your hands full.'

He gathered up the page and put it on the bench with the rest, weighing it all down with a big stone he found at the edge of the lawn.

'Thank you, Chief Inspector,' she said.

'I don't go by my official title when I'm off duty,' he told her. He held out a hand. 'Mal Mitchell.'

They shook hands.

'I'm Pamela. But I suppose you know that already. From your files.'

He shrugged. 'I try not to memorise every name I come across.'

'I thought police officers remembered everything.'

'Only if it's relevant… I'm surprised you've come here, in the circumstances.'

'Paul and I had already decided to move here, before…'

'Yes, you told us that at the time. But I suppose it's as well to face up to these things.'

'It wasn't a case of facing up to anything,' she said sharply. 'We were nearly at the point of no return with the sale of our flat by the time Paul… I couldn't cope with the hassle of pulling out.'

He nodded, almost as if he understood, although she doubted if anybody could possibly understand.

'Do you know anybody who could fix the gate and the fences?' she enquired, desperate to change the subject. He probably shouldn't even be talking to her about it. As she understood it, there was still a chance there would be a Fatal Accident Inquiry into Paul's death, and surely the police would be involved in that. She shivered suddenly, and stroked Tiger's head to give her hands something to do.

'We get cards through the door sometimes from people who do that kind of thing,' he said amicably. 'I'll fish one out for you. If you have any trouble with them just let me know. I believe there are local groups on social media too, where you can get recommendations.'

'Thank you,' she said. She glanced back at the letter. 'I'd better go inside with the dogs for now.'

'I'll do a temporary fix on the side gate if you like,' he said.

'That would be great, thanks.'

She was irrationally annoyed with herself for not having known he lived next-door. But how could she have known? She and Paul had only visited the bungalow once, and she hadn't bothered to come down here again for a second look, or hadn't wanted to, after his death.

She carried Tiger into the house, Lily following them in, and shut them in the front room before returning to pick up the lawyer's letter. But instead of reading it, she sat for a while on her second-favourite chair, staring blankly at the blank wall where she intended to put a painting she and Paul had once bought at an art fair in the days when they went to these events together, and remembering the interviews she'd endured with the police during the days after his death. Detective Chief Inspector Mitchell had presided over one of the sessions. His manner hadn't been aggressive, exactly, but she had found the whole experience intimidating in itself. She had almost believed by the end of it that she herself had something to hide, despite having a cast-iron alibi for several days around the time of Paul's death. Her mother had been terminally ill and she had spent these days waiting in a hospital at the other end of the country, with no possible opportunity to get back to Edinburgh in between times.

She had wondered occasionally, in the early hours of some morning or other in the few weeks that followed both deaths, if the police suspected her of paying somebody to arrange Paul's death and if that was why they'd been looking for a motive on her part. In any case she appeared to have convinced them she had nothing to do with it. They hadn't interviewed her again, anyway. She knew nothing about any subsequent investigations or what would come of the Procurator Fiscal's involvement.

Her favourite chair now evidently belonged to the two dogs. They did look quite sweet, lying close together, their heads up and their expressions quizzical. She had a sudden urge to sketch them like that. But if she went to the studio to find paper and pencils, would they move and spoil the composition?

It was easier just to sit and watch them for a while. A sketch she made of them like this would be too chocolate-boxy for words in any case, though she might have been able to use it in a children's storybook.

Her thoughts returned to the police and whether they would ever reach any conclusion about Paul's death. There were so many problematic aspects to it, although this was the first time she'd really been able to bring herself to consider them. Why had he even been there on the causeway in the dark, with the tide coming in? Had he intended to drown himself, and if so, weren't there less bizarre ways of doing it? He could have swum out into the Forth and let the current carry him away, or walked to Cramond Island at low tide and jumped off a rock at the far side, assuming the water was deep enough to drown in at that time of day. It would certainly have been cold enough. He hadn't had to stand on the causeway waiting for the tide to overcome him…

The idea of it made her shiver, as she had known it would, which was why she didn't often let her mind wander this far. Up to now she had usually been able to divert her thoughts into other, more comfortable channels when they seemed to be straying in that direction. She would either find something practical to do or watch another wildlife documentary on television. It was all that policeman's fault. Why did he have to live next-door and not somewhere else? Portobello. Aberdeen. Norwich. Anywhere else but here.

She jumped up from the chair, and sure enough, the two dogs followed her through to the studio. Was there really any point in trying for a sketch now? Maybe she should have pencils and paper in every room in case they did something cute when she wasn't expecting it.

Pamela laughed at herself, which she took as a positive sign. She might even risk going back to the beach at Silverknowes the following day. Surely she wouldn't be unlucky enough to meet that woman again. Even if she did, where was the harm in exchanging a few words with a fellow dog-walker? It was about time she got to know a few new people. She had to start somewhere.

Chapter 4 Crossed Paths

'... so that was why I wondered about the dogs,' said Caitlin French earnestly.

'Yes, of course, I understand why you'd wonder about them,' said Pamela.

'But you got them from the boy. I should've known that... Only why did he bring them to you in the first place? Had you met him before?'

Pamela shook her head. She didn't want to explain to this woman, almost a stranger, the feeling of familiarity she had experienced on seeing the boy on her door-step.

They had met again down on the promenade – of course – and this time, because the weather was still warm and sunny, they'd gone along to the café and sat at a table outside so that they could keep the dogs close by. Tiger had shown signs of wanting to play with Darren, who showed a good turn of speed once he got going – maybe there was some greyhound in Caitlin's dog's dubious ancestry, Pamela thought - but Lily was still hesitant. Pamela sympathised with that. She was hesitant too about getting to know Caitlin. But the woman had an air of fragility about her, of anxiously wanting to be liked, and it was almost impossible to deliver a rebuff that might send her over the edge into an old-fashioned decline.

The boy who had given her the dogs had been a neighbour of Caitlin's. Or his mother had been a friend of hers. The words had poured out so quickly that Pamela hadn't been sure she was keeping up with the story.

Caitlin suddenly leaned forward and put her hand on top of Pamela's where it lay on the table.

'I was there, you know. When his mother died.'

'Oh, dear,' said Pamela.

At that moment she wished she had resisted the temptation to return to the promenade. She should have known she would bump into this woman again, and she really didn't think she wanted to hear this particular story.

'It was on the crossing,' Caitlin went on. 'That's where I work. It's only part-time, of course, but it fits in with the dog and everything, and I like to see the kids… The car just came out of nowhere and hit her. It would've been me too except that I had turned round to make sure everybody was across. It might have been one of them. It was horrible…'

She gave a theatrical shudder, or at least Pamela thought there was a touch of the theatre about it.

'Don't go on unless you want to,' she said. She wasn't squeamish exactly, but she thought this woman might be the kind to go into excruciating detail about injuries and so on.

'It's all right,' said Caitlin. 'I think it helps me a bit. Every time I go over it, I feel a wee bit better after.'

That was all very well, but the person she told about it might feel worse. Pamela remained silent this time. Caitlin took that as a signal to continue.

'I knew right away she wasn't going to make it. There was a woman who'd just been waiting to cross who knew first aid, though, so I left her to that. I gave some man who was passing my lollipop to stop all the traffic while I got the others to wait on the pavement out of the way and called an ambulance.' She shook her head. 'Poor Joanne.'

'You knew them quite well, then?' said Pamela.

She wanted to get up and leave without hearing any more, but somehow it was impossible, with the woman pouring her heart out. Why did people do that with complete strangers? Unless maybe it was easier that way than talking to your nearest and dearest. Hmm. She frowned, wondering if she should try it some time. Not with Caitlin though – the woman obviously had enough disturbing memories of her own.

'They lived just the other side of the main road from me. They hadn't always been there – I think they moved from Glasgow or somewhere. But I met Joanne at my Zumba class, and I saw Andy on school days for a while, crossing the road at that very same place... I don't know what she was doing on the crossing that day, though. She used to always catch the bus from her own side of the road.'

'When was it? The accident, I mean?' asked Pamela.

Caitlin shrugged. 'A month or so back.'

'I suppose it's taken him since then to realise he couldn't cope with the dogs,' said Pamela thoughtfully.

'Oh yes – the dogs. Maybe that was it. I think he's got college or something now. He'll maybe have moved into some student flat or a bedsitter where he can't keep animals.' Caitlin didn't sound convinced, but at least she didn't seem suspicious any longer about Pamela's acquisition of the dogs. 'Are you sure you didn't know them before?' she added.

Pamela shook her head. 'I definitely didn't. What was the last name again?'

'Hutchison, it was. Joanne and Andy Hutchison... If you see Andy again, tell him I was asking for him.'

Had the father not been about anywhere? Not that a single-parent family was all that unusual these days.

Caitlin suddenly gulped down the rest of her hot chocolate and stood up. 'Sorry – I'll have to get going. Nearly time for the wee ones to come out.'

'Oh, yes,' said Pamela. 'Sorry to have kept you so long.'

'That's all right. Maybe see you again some time.'

The woman untied her dog's lead from the table leg and set off up the slope towards the road. Pamela was glad there hadn't been time to offer her a lift. She hadn't really found her way around here, although it didn't seem too complicated. Getting down to the promenade and back was about it so far.

Joanne and Andy Hutchison. No, the names didn't ring any bells. And yet her own name must have somehow been familiar to Andy, at least.

Pamela came back to reality with a jolt when the yapping began.

A stranger had picked up Tiger and was carrying him away from the table. Lily whined in sympathy, but she had wedged herself up against Pamela's legs again and wouldn't have made an easy target. Pamela jumped to her feet, untied the dog's leads and picked up Lily, and raced after the man. He broke into a run, heading up the slope where Caitlin had just gone, up to the road with all its parked cars. What if he got Tiger into his car and drove off? What on earth would she do?

Panic weakened her legs, and she didn't think she had any chance of catching up with him, but just as she felt the first silly tears start into her eyes, Tiger wriggled free and scurried back down the slope towards her, yapping either in greeting or alarm, she wasn't sure which. She bent and got hold of his collar as he reached her so that she could clip his lead back into place.

It was only then that she realised she'd been yelling at the top of her voice at the abductor throughout the pursuit. Other people using the path were giving her strange looks and a wide berth. Still, that didn't matter now that she had both dogs. She put Lily down and the two of them greeted each other, tails wagging fast.

The stranger reached the top of the slope and vanished without looking back. She hoped he got himself well out of the way. She didn't want to risk a confrontation when she was putting the dogs in the car. And what it he hid somewhere up there and jumped out at her?

She told herself not to be silly. It was bright daylight, and there were other people around. Surely he wouldn't risk being caught, or the police being called.

A large, dark green car shot past her just as she emerged at the top of the slope. Maybe that had been him.

Knowing he was unlikely to do anything more for the moment was fine in theory, but she had a good look round when she reached the road, and kept looking round as she walked along to her car. She supposed that was what DCI Mitchell would have advised, had she asked him. If he even concerned himself with crimes that hadn't even happened yet but were all in her imagination, that was.

Chapter 5 More about Andy

Pamela avoided Silverknowes promenade for the next few days. In any case, a north wind had arrived, apparently blowing straight from the Arctic, which would have made what she already thought of as her usual walk particularly unpleasant. Instead she left the bungalow on foot, for a change on the first day, and made for the riverside walk, but without venturing as far as the mouth of the Almond, which she knew was too close for comfort to the causeway and the island it led to.

Lily was left exhausted, presumably because of having to climb a steep flight of steps on the way up the river, so the following day Pamela relented and drove them all to a nearby woodland area, which seemed to get the seal of approval from both dogs.

Towards the end of a week that was starting to seem endless, Pamela got a pleasant surprise one morning when she answered her phone.

'Hello, stranger!' said a cheerful voice. 'How did it go with the move?'

'Kim - hi! Thanks – it's going to be fine.'

'Going to be?'

'Oh well, I suppose the move went OK. Something weird happened, though.'

'Really?' said Kim. 'Tell me more!'

'I think you should come and see for yourself,' said Pamela. She glanced at the chaos in the front room, where she had only just got round to starting to unpack the boxes of books. Tiger was currently chewing up one of Paul's conspiracy theory books, but that was all right with her.

'I thought you'd never ask,' said Kim. 'When do you want me? I can jump on a bus right now if you like.'

'Give me time to clear a space for you to sit down.'

They agreed on Friday afternoon. Pamela felt energised by the call. She hadn't liked to lean on her friends too heavily over the past few difficult months, but she wasn't going to turn Kim Fitzpatrick away either. They had been through quite a lot together, and although they hadn't seen each other for ages – it must be nearly a year, apart from Paul's funeral, when they hadn't really had time to talk properly – she knew they would be able to pick up where they'd left off. As far as she could recall, that must have been about the time of Kim's second divorce. They would have a lot to share.

She smiled to herself as she unpacked the top layer of the next box. Mostly Paul's sci-fi. What had happened to her own books? She stuffed the sci-fi collection into the nearest shelf without even looking at the titles. She could always sort everything out later.

In a sudden burst of energy, Lily jumped into the box and settled down on the next layer of books.

Pamela sighed. Tiger glanced up from the conspiracy book, his ears pricked up as if he knew what was coming next before she did. Maybe if she tired the dogs out with a long walk she'd be able to get down to some serious unpacking afterwards.

Had Tiger planted that idea in her mind? Was she actually letting a small terrier control her movements? Things would have to change, otherwise she would never get any real work done again and she might as well convert her studio to a spare bedroom and let it out to tourists.

With this dire thought in mind, she found herself driving round to Silverknowes, telling herself that the chances of bumping into Caitlin French yet again must surely be miniscule. In any case, if she did happen to see the woman, she could either turn and walk in the other direction or make some excuse to avoid having to speak to her for long. She certainly didn't want to find herself getting too friendly with Caitlin. She had never trusted people who shared too much information too quickly. Was that irrational? Or simply a rational defence against these people who went off and shared everything with the next person they met?

Pamela was still trying to tell herself not to be so judgemental as she set off down the slope to the promenade, clutching the dogs' leads tightly. There was no way she was going to let them off the lead yet, no matter how hard Tiger tugged.

As usual, she turned to go in the opposite direction from the island and the causeway. She would have to look at them on the way back, of course, but that couldn't be helped. She would just give all her attention to the task of not falling over the dogs or getting the leads in a tangle, and she wouldn't look straight ahead unless she had to. That strategy would have the advantage that she could plausibly claim not to have seen Caitlin French.

Lily had started to pull at the lead on these last few walks and Pamela even allowed herself to hope the dog wasn't really as nervy as she had seemed at the beginning. Tiger, of course, had never shown any sign of nerves, unless his propensity to find ways out of the garden had signified that he was panicking about being in a new place.

Soon after she had turned back towards the café and her parking spot, Tiger demonstrated his lack of clinginess by pulling so hard on the lead that the other end flew out of her hand and he scampered away, moving a good bit faster than a dog with such short legs should be able to move.

She tried calling his name, not that he had shown any sign of recognising it the last few times. Instead he picked up his pace and seemed to be heading towards some complete stranger who was walking towards them. He didn't seem to have a dog with him. Was he the evil abductor from a few days before?

Pamela had a moment's panic, but Tiger was wagging his tail frantically, and when he reached the stranger he jumped up and down in excitement. The man leaned down and tickled his ears, which drove the dog into further expressions of ecstasy.

'I'm sorry,' gasped Pamela as she and Lily approached them. 'He seems to think... Oh! It's you!'

The stranger wasn't a complete stranger after all.

'Mrs Prendergast,' said the boy, Andy, in a flat tone.

She wondered what would happen if she called him by the name she had learnt from Caitlin French. Maybe better not.

'Are they behaving themselves?' he asked.

Lily tugged at the lead, trying to get closer to him. Pamela relaxed her grip just a fraction so that he could at least give the dog a pat.

'Would you care if they weren't?' she countered.

'I do care what happens to them,' he said. 'That's why I left them with you.'

'But you don't know me! For all you knew, I might have taken them straight to the dog and car home. Or let them wander off and get lost.'

'I didn't think you would.'

'Caitlin French was asking for you,' she said, hoping to surprise him. He wasn't the only one who could be cryptic.

He started back. 'You know Caitlin French, do you?'

He didn't sound altogether impressed.

She shrugged. 'The dogs introduced us. She recognised them.'

'I suppose she told you my name, then.'

'Andy Hutchison. You don't mind me knowing it, do you?'

He shrugged.

'What are you doing down here anyway? It's quite a way from the New Town.'

'I live here now,' she told him. She wasn't going to give away her actual address, of course, but there was no point in pretending she hadn't moved house.

'Here?' He smiled and waved his hand in a big sweep. 'What do you mean, here? Why did you have to go and move?'

'It was moving day when you came round with the dogs… I don't even know how you found me at that address. Or why.'

He sighed, staring into the distance for a few moments. A plane descended, somewhere above their heads. She was reluctant to ask him any direct questions. He was as nervy as Lily was, in his own way.

'It's a long story,' he said at last.

'Come on, then. We'd better get ourselves a coffee – or would you prefer tea? Or hot chocolate?'

Responding to her brisk tone, he agreed to a hot chocolate but turned down the offer of a scone.

'I found your address in my mum's old address book,' he said abruptly once they had sat down, again at an outside table.

Pamela stared at the boy. 'What was she doing with my address?'

He shrugged. 'It was only after – after the accident. I was going through her things, with my friend's mum. I looked you up after that. Online. You seemed like the kind of person who might be good with dogs.'

How on earth had he pieced that idea together from the fragments of her life that were visible online?

She wondered if he had any family of his own now. Going through his mum's things didn't seem like the kind of activity that a stranger should be helping with. What about his father? He must have had one at some time, even if they had never even met each other. There might have been aunts and uncles, cousins…

He glanced up at her and she thought for a moment that he could tell what she was thinking. But it was probably just a trick of the light that made his gaze seem somehow harder and more knowing than they should have been at his age. She wished, stupidly, that they were having a drink together in some dim bar in the city centre instead of out here. The light was stark and clear, making it hard to hide anything.

'Did Caitlin French tell you what happened? To my mum, I mean?'

'Yes.' Pamela didn't want the boy to have to go over it again. 'An accident on the crossing.'

He nodded. 'I don't even know why she was there in the first place. She always caught the bus from our side of the road.'

That was exactly what Caitlin had said.

'Maybe she saw a friend and wanted to speak to them,' suggested Pamela.

'But then she would've missed her bus and been late for work... She didn't have many friends about here, anyway. We've only been in Edinburgh less than a year.'

'She knew Caitlin French.'

'They weren't exactly friends, though. They sometimes bumped into each other walking the dogs, that's all.'

'Did Caitlin tell you any more about what happened that day?'

He nodded. 'Mum was talking on her mobile. I suppose she wasn't paying attention.'

'Oh dear,' said Pamela inadequately.

'I guess the police thought it was partly her own fault. But the car was definitely going too fast as well.'

'Some people just ignore the twenty-mile limit.'

He nodded.

'You'd think somebody might have described the car,' added Pamela. 'Or they would've maybe seen the number-plate.'

'Probably going too fast,' said Andy. He drained his mug suddenly, and got to his feet. 'Better get going, then. It was good to see the dogs. Thanks for looking after them,' he added awkwardly. 'I didn't know what else to do. I couldn't stay in the house where we were, and I've got college classes a lot of the time.'

'Are you studying for a qualification?' said Pamela, hoping she didn't sound too much like a careers adviser.

'Oh, just Highers at the moment,' he said. 'Exams coming up soon, too… Maybe see you around some time.'

He was gone then, running up the slope to the road as if pursued by a pack of hounds. He was very nearly pursued by Tiger and Lily, who put all their efforts into freeing the leads from the table leg. Pamela grabbed Tiger's lead just as he was about to bound off into the distance too.

'No, you don't!'

He gave her an aggrieved look.

Pamela realised as she walked at a more sensible pace back up to the car that her conversation with Andy had given her more questions than answers. It was the address book that worried her most, but she also turned over in her mind why Joanne Hutchison had crossed the road that day instead of catching her usual bus and whether Andy did have any living relatives to turn to. Of course it wasn't up to her to find answers to any of these questions except possibly the first of them, but she couldn't help feeling they might all be connected, part of a larger puzzle.

She made a quick sketch of the boy when she got home. The sense of familiarity had only grown stronger with their second meeting.

Chapter 6 In the Box

There was work to be done – Pamela had a commission for illustrations for a children's book, not the toddler kind with furry animals that spoke and railway engines with faces, but a slightly more advanced one about race and diversity. They were mostly like that these days. Sometimes she longed to be able to draw children going off on their own and having adventures, but she told herself sternly that people didn't write that kind of nonsense any longer, and a good thing too.

By the end of Friday morning she was tired of trying to follow the instructions she'd received from the publisher, and decided she deserved a change of activity. This was when she appreciated being a freelancer who decided her own working hours and who could afford to turn down commissions on occasion too. The lawyers hadn't worked out the value of Paul's estate yet, but Pamela had inherited some money from her mother not long before her husband's death, so she could wait.

She decided to choose a box at random, bring it into her studio and unpack it, come what may, before Kim arrived in mid-afternoon. In a way she hoped it would be a box of her mother's ornaments and vases, which she could reasonably donate to a charity shop, and not old paperwork, which she would feel bound to go through before discarding. She shut the dogs into the front room. They'd had a quick walk earlier, and she was hoping Kim might agree to another one later on.

As soon as she opened the box, which was stacked with the other non-urgent items left over from the move, she knew it didn't contain anything of her mother's.

This box had been sent over from Paul's studio in Glasgow in response to an email she'd sent them enquiring about the contents of the place. She had been mildly surprised that there was only one box – and not a very big one either – but maybe there was more to come, and she wasn't in any hurry to take delivery of any jewellery-making tools and the like.

There was a note on top of everything. She read it with increasing puzzlement.

'Mrs Prendergast – this is all that was left after Paul moved out. I think we've got it all, but please get in touch again if you were expecting anything else. We can have another look round. Regards, Steve.'

'After Paul moved out'. What was that supposed to mean? She took the note and placed it carefully on the desk.

As far as she knew, Paul hadn't exactly moved out of his Glasgow studio, unless that was some sort of weird euphemism for death. He'd lived in Glasgow during the week purely so that he could work all hours at the studio. They had really only seen each other at weekends. The arrangement suited them both, as they had never been the kind to cling to each other. They had different sets of friends, or at least she thought he had friends over in the west although she hadn't enquired about them, and they each had different interests and thriving careers of their own. There were no kids to worry about, and Pamela had never missed having a man constantly under her feet – not that she wasn't always pleased to see him on Friday evening, or sometimes Saturday at lunchtime. They enjoyed at least one date night every weekend, and she had fondly imagined their relationship was better for the time spent apart.

Why hadn't he told her about moving out of the studio? Even if he'd only moved down the road into a different place, it seemed very odd.

She decided she'd have to contact the lawyers about this, but not now. Better to wait until after the weekend, when the information would have had time to sink in and she might even manage to string a sentence together coherently.

For now she would simply unpack this box as planned and then file away the contents somewhere, to be forgotten about for the moment and maybe considered again at some future time when her feelings were a bit less raw.

The first thing she came to after setting the note aside was a framed copy of their wedding photo. She had never liked it much. She didn't like the way they'd done her hair, and she had felt silly even at the time wearing a white dress and a lacy veil. It was so unlike her usual style, which was sleek and minimalist. That was what she tended to aim for, anyway.

Encouraging, though, that he had kept a copy in his studio. She imagined him glancing at it from time to time as he worked, possibly even inspired by something about the picture… no, not really.

She put the photo on the desk, next to the note, and was about to delve further into the box when the door-bell rang.

'Sorry I'm a bit early,' said Kim when Pamela opened the door. 'I just managed to catch the bus before the one I meant to get. It seemed silly to let it go past. I didn't think you'd mind.'

'It's lovely to see you!' said Pamela, giving her friend a quick hug. They weren't really the hugging kind, either of them, but somehow the circumstances demanded a show of affection.

'So, how is the new house?'

'Fine. I'm afraid I haven't finished unpacking yet, though, so it's a bit messy.'

'You've only been here a week or so, haven't you? That's nothing! Plenty of time to get yourself sorted out. Have you chosen a studio? Or is there one in the garden?'

'That would have been nice,' Pamela agreed. 'But a bit redundant, since it's only me here. You can have a look at the studio, but I haven't got it completely set up yet.'

'Nice view of the garden,' Kim remarked when they were in the room. She turned away from the window and glanced down at the desk-top. She picked up the wedding picture. 'You and Paul? What a crazy veil!'

'Yes – I was just thinking that too,' said Pamela, laughing.

Kim glanced at the sketch of Andy Hutchison, which was propped against the desk tidy. She reached out and picked it up for a closer look.

'Who's this?'

Pamela instantly wished she had shoved the thing in a drawer. She had meant to clear the desk-top before Kim arrived.

'Just somebody I've met.'

'Hmm… He's got a look of Paul about him – I wondered if he was maybe a nephew or something.'

'I don't think Paul has any nephews,' Pamela replied without really thinking. 'Just a couple of nieces, as far as I know. But we never see – never saw them. They live in Sussex. Or is it Suffolk? Somewhere on the English coast, anyway.'

'Hmm,' said Kim again, but she replaced the sketch where she had found it.

'Let's get ourselves a cup of coffee – or would you rather have tea? I've got some pastries. There's a nice little shop just up the road a bit.'

'By the traffic lights?'

'No, the other way. Come and see what you think of the kitchen. Paul really liked it. That was one reason for buying the house.'

'Did he plan to spend more time in Edinburgh once you'd moved?' asked Kim, once they had collected their coffee and pastries and moved into the front room. The dogs greeted them both with equal enthusiasm as long-lost friends. Even Lily took to Kim at once, and curled up by her feet.

'I don't know,' said Pamela. 'He was keen to move out of the New Town anyway. I didn't really mind either way myself, but now that I'm here I'm finding it quite relaxing. But it's partly the dogs – I'm walking every day with them, and I think that's good for me.'

'It probably is,' agreed Kim. 'What made you decide to acquire those two? I don't remember you being a dog person up to now.'

'Well, it was a bit strange,' said Pamela.

She explained how the dogs had come into her possession, and Kim listened, eyes wide in disbelief.

'Didn't you even think of taking them to the nearest police station?' she said. 'They might have been stolen. Maybe they're chipped, and you could find the real owners.'

Pamela felt an unexpected pang of something at the idea of giving up Tiger and Lily. She hadn't even considered that they might have been stolen. But in any case, the dogs had recognised Andy, and even Lily, with her suspicious mind, had greeted him like a long-lost friend. She explained her latest encounter with him to Kim, leaving out the details of Andy's mother's death.

'It all sounds a bit weird to me,' said Kim. 'Are you sure you really want to have anything to do with those people? Even if this boy does look like Paul.'

Pamela wished Kim hadn't repeated her comment about the sketch. Thinking about the supposed likeness made her feel very uneasy.

'There aren't any people. I mean, it's just him. Andy Hutchison.'

'What about the woman? You said she knew the dogs too.'

'Never mind the woman!' Pamela spoke more sharply than she had meant to.

Kim held up a hand. 'Sorry. I can see you don't want to give the dogs up. They'll be company for you.'

'Yes,' said Pamela. She remembered something else, something she hoped would take Kim's mind off the dogs. 'I suppose I could ask my next-door neighbour about them. He's a policeman. But he probably doesn't have anything to do with stolen dogs. He's a bit higher up than that.'

'Ooh, exciting!' said Kim. 'A detective?'

'Yes. A detective chief inspector.'

'Married? Children?'

'For goodness' sake, Kim!' Pamela had to laugh. 'I don't know. If he does have children, they've been very quiet so far. And invisible.'

After the pastries were gone, Kim sat back in the chair and asked,

'How are you getting on – really?'

'I'm fine,' said Pamela. 'Or at least I'm well on the way to being fine. I'm really glad I carried on with the move. If I'd stayed where I was, it would have been harder to accept the other changes.'

'Paul had a studio in Glasgow, didn't he?'

'Well, I thought so. I mean, he did have a studio there, and a small flat. It's a bit of a puzzle though – there wasn't as much stuff in the studio as I'd expected. He seems to have moved into a different place at some point, but I didn't know that until now.'

'Literally now, you mean?'

'I opened the box minutes before you rang the door-bell. There was a note on top. That was the first I'd heard of him moving out of the place.'

'But – why wouldn't he tell you about it?' asked Kim.

'I don't know,' said Pamela.

She wished now that she hadn't opened that particular box today. She would have preferred to have more time to digest the information in the note before talking to her friend about it, and she wasn't ready to deal with Kim's questions.

'Would you like to see the garden?' she said.

'Only if your policeman happens to be looking over the fence,' said Kim, fluttering her eyelashes.

Pamela ignored this and led the way through the kitchen and out. The dogs followed, of course. She picked up Tiger, who wriggled and whined.

'Maybe I'd better shut them indoors,' she said.

'Oh, don't do that – they'll enjoy the fresh air,' said Kim.

Pamela was all too conscious that she hadn't found anybody to mend the fence properly yet. Oh well, she'd just have to hope her temporary repairs lasted a little longer. She placed Tiger on the ground again and said to him sternly, 'No naughty tricks this time!'

He ran straight over to the place where he'd got through the last time, of course, but this time he turned away, disappointed. She went over to have a look and found the gap had been covered up with quite a solid-looking repair. The chief inspector must have done that himself. She wasn't sure how she felt about that, but there was no doubt that Tiger wouldn't be able to push, slither or wriggle his way through.

'There's plenty of scope,' said Kim. 'Maybe you could have a wee summer-house down at the end there, or a gazebo. And how about some of those raised beds?'

'I'm not quite at the stage of needing raised beds yet,' said Pamela, amused rather than annoyed with her friend this time. 'Give it a few years.'

They walked down to the end of the garden and Kim peered over the fence.

'Maybe you could walk the dogs over there,' she reported. 'There's grass and woodland.'

'It probably belongs to somebody,' said Pamela. 'Almost everywhere does. Or maybe it's part of a golf course. That's always a possibility too.'

'Have you thought of taking up golf?' Kim enquired as they walked slowly back towards the house. 'That'd be a good way of meeting new people.'

She meant new men, of course. Pamela decided to go on the attack.

'How about you, Kim? Have you met any new people lately?'

Kim blushed and mumbled.

It took the rest of her visit for Pamela to get anything out of her. When she did, she realised Kim had only got in touch in the first place because she had confidences to impart. At least imparting them distracted her friend from asking any more awkward questions.

Pamela desperately needed time to think, and not about whether to have a summer-house or a gazebo either. There would be time enough for that kind of decision later.

Chapter 7 The Glasgow Mystery

'We were just about to write to you about that.'

'Oh, really?' said Pamela sceptically.

As planned, she had called her lawyers as soon as they opened for business on Monday.

'Yes, really,' said the youngest in the firm, an acquaintance of hers who had dealt expeditiously enough with her mother's estate but who appeared to be making Paul's financial affairs more complicated than was necessary at this point. 'Were you not aware that he sold the Glasgow flat some time ago?'

'Some time ago? How much time are we talking about?'

'Oh, three years or so,' said the lawyer casually. She must have known this information would cause the ground to shake under Pamela's feet, but that knowledge wasn't evident in her tone.

'Three years? Give me a minute... Three whole years? But where – what was he thinking? Where did he go?'

'He didn't tell you, then.'

'No, he bloody well didn't! Sorry – I know it isn't your fault. The place was in his name of course. He must have got somebody else to handle the sale. But that isn't illegal – is it?'

Pamela thought she heard a muffled laugh at the other end of the line.

'Not illegal – but a bit odd, in the circumstances. I mean, as far as you were concerned he still stayed there during the week.'

'I suppose he bought a different flat in Glasgow, then,' said Pamela. 'It wouldn't have made any difference to the way we organised things. I'm just surprised he didn't say anything.'

'It makes a difference to the amount you might expect to end up with. From his estate, that is. Unless we can track down some other property he bought in the mean-time.'

'Well, maybe if you had some contacts in Glasgow,' Pamela began.

'We have an office there,' said the woman. 'But we'd have known about this sooner if he'd used them for any subsequent property transactions.'

'He moved out of his studio too,' said Pamela. 'That's what made me think of calling you.'

'I see,' said the lawyer after a pause. 'Have you thought that perhaps he re-located? Moved to somewhere completely different? Perhaps the rent was too high in the centre of Glasgow or something.'

'He was a high-end jewellery designer,' said Pamela. 'He could afford the rent. We shared the expenses of the Edinburgh flat, and it was in both our names, as you know.'

'I suppose I could ask around and see if my colleagues over in the west know anything,' the lawyer offered at last. 'I'll get back to you as soon as I have any relevant information.'

'Thank you. I'm afraid this is turning out to be a bit more complicated than I had thought it was.'

After she had ended the call, Pamela wondered why her own tone had been so apologetic. Presumably lawyers thrived on these complicated cases. They would be paid more at the end of the day. And they had no emotional involvement either. It was all business to them. Whereas to her… It was past time to take the dogs out.

She didn't have the energy to think of anywhere else to go, so she drove round to Silverknowes, hoping not to meet either of the two people she had previously met there. Surely on a Monday morning they had something better to do than to hang about the promenade waiting for the chance to torment her?

Not that either of them had set out to torment her, she told herself. It had just happened that way. But today she didn't want to be bothered with other people's problems. She had more than enough of her own to cope with.

For a while it seemed as if she might be in luck. There were fewer cars parked there than usual, and the promenade was near enough deserted. It was because of this that she was hesitant about going round the corner into the next little bay, but turned back before she'd got very far and forced herself instead to walk towards the island for longer. The tide was in and the island appeared small and innocuous under the blue sky. Had Paul been trying to reach the island that night? Or had he misjudged the tide times and tried to get back to the mainland when it was too late?

Pamela thought they would probably never know one way or the other.

She was about to turn up a path she'd seen that looked as if it might be a short-cut back to the car when somebody called her name.

'Mrs Prendergast!'

It was Andy Hutchison, and he was waving rather desperately as he hurried towards her.

'Just a minute! Please!'

So much for avoiding other people's problems, she thought wryly, coming to a standstill at the foot of the path. Tiger strained towards Andy, while Lily made little whining sounds which seemed to be an expression of great excitement.

'I don't have much time,' Pamela lied. Actually she had been avoiding people so assiduously for a few days that she was well ahead on her commissions, and the only prospect that awaited her at home was the unpacking of more boxes. Or working her way down what she thought of as Paul's box. Who knew what unwelcome secrets she might uncover there?

'I've spoken to somebody else,' he said breathlessly. 'The woman who tried to save my mum's life. She remembered the car. I've got something to take to the police.'

'Great,' said Pamela, wondering what this had to do with her.

'I need somebody to go with me.'

'What about this woman? They'll need her statement, won't they?'

He grimaced. The sense of familiarity grew abruptly stronger.

'She won't talk to the police.'

'Or you could ask Caitlin French? She was there, wasn't she?'

'No way,' he said quite definitely. 'She didn't even want to talk to the first constable who came along that day, only she must have known she had to wait for the police or they'd track her down and make trouble. I guess she thinks she's done her bit already… Can you come with me?'

'But it's really nothing to do with me!' she protested.

'Your name was in my mum's address book. It must mean something.'

'I don't know why that should be, but I really don't think.... And what you've got to tell them is just hearsay, isn't it? They probably won't take any notice.'

'I really need to do this,' said Andy.

He turned away from her and his shoulders slumped.

'If we could think of any reason for me to come with you, I'd come,' she said recklessly.

'We know there's some connection,' said Andy. 'Don't you want to know what it is? Maybe we can find out, between us.'

Pamela wanted to tell him her life was complicated enough without her involvement in a hit and run case as well as a possible fatal accident inquiry, but she hesitated for a little too long, and he added,

'We've got the dogs to connect us now, anyway. That's like being family.'

He looked at her so hopefully, and he was so young, that she gave in. He must have known she would, after being a soft touch with the dogs.

'Oh, all right then, I suppose I could come with you to the police,' she said. 'Just don't expect me to say anything much. I'm only there as a kind of concerned friend. Or something.'

'Concerned friend, yes,' he said. 'Can we go tomorrow?'

'I suppose we might as well get it over with,' she said. 'Where's the police station?'

They worked out a meeting place and the route to the police station, and exchanged mobile numbers. Afterwards, when she was driving home, she thought it might have been better just to approach DCI Mitchell informally. But then again, maybe he didn't want to be bothered with work in his spare time.

Chapter 8 Reluctant Friend

They had run through what they planned to say to the police beforehand, but when it came to the point Pamela thought it seemed ridiculously thin and unconvincing, and she could see that the police officers they spoke to were wondering what she was doing there. On the other hand, if it had been Andy on his own they might not have listened as politely as they did.

'So what are you saying?' said the woman officer, who hadn't been quite as dismissive as the men. 'Do you think we haven't even tried to find the car that ran over your mum?'

'No, it isn't that,' said Andy, but he glanced over at Pamela as if asking for help.

'I think Mr Hutchison thought having a better description of the car might help with your enquiries,' said Pamela. 'He wasn't sure if you'd already spoken to the woman concerned.'

'We did speak to her at the scene,' said the other officer, a young man. He flicked a cardboard file open and stared at the single piece of paper inside. 'She was still in shock – didn't remember anything about the car then... I'm surprised she's remembered now, after all this time.'

'She said she saw one like it speeding along Ferry Road, and that brought it back to her,' said Andy.

'The chances of tracking it down from this new description, though...' The officer closed the file again. 'We'd need more than this to go on. And even if we find the car, we'd have no real evidence that the driver was speeding. Just some people's opinions. The speed cameras haven't been working on that stretch for a while.'

'Shouldn't you get them working again, then?' said Pamela, unable to resist commenting. 'Before this happens to somebody else?'

'Different department,' said the male officer. He shook his head. 'Nothing more to be done.'

'What if it turned out to be something different?' suggested Pamela. 'Not an accident, I mean. The driver deliberately targeting Mrs Hutchison.'

She had no idea where this came from. The two officers stared at her as if she'd thrown off her clothes and run out into the street screaming blue murder. Andy's expression wasn't much different from theirs.

'What did you say that for?' he hissed as they walked back out to the car. 'There's no way anybody would want to run down my mum.'

'I don't know. I'm sorry.'

She got into the driving seat and waited for a few moments before even turning the engine on.

There were some things bothering her about Joanne Hutchison's death. The reason for her to cross the road. The fact that she was apparently talking on her mobile as she crossed. As a driver, Pamela knew this second point was not particularly unusual, but what if somebody had called her, summoning her to the other side of the road, and kept her talking as she crossed to make sure she wouldn't be looking around for speeding cars? Then there was the dog thief incident, and the fact that Andy had found her own name in Joanne Hutchison's address book, something that was still to be explained.

'Don't be so silly,' she told herself, only realising she'd spoken the words aloud when she noticed the way Andy was looking at her. 'Sorry – I was just putting two and two together and making about fifteen.'

He frowned. 'I thought the police might be more interested in the description of the car… Oh, well. I suppose that's that. Sorry to have bothered you.'

'It was no bother,' said Pamela. She pulled away from the kerb at last. 'Shouldn't you be at college? Can I drop you off somewhere?'

'I'm skiving off today,' he told her. 'It's fine,' he added quickly. 'The exams are coming up and we don't have so many classes just now. I'll walk back from Cramond if you want to drop me somewhere. Thanks for coming with me anyway.'

She did as he asked, and watched him take the turning towards the shore. Maybe she should have warned him about the tides on the causeway. But he must know about them already, having lived not far away for a while…

She turned round in the next side road and went back to find him. He had already reached the entrance to the church and the remains of the Roman fort. She stopped on the wrong side of the road for a moment and opened her window.

'Take care. You've got to watch out for the tide if you're crossing to the island. It comes in really quickly.'

He gave her a funny look, very similar to the one he had given her in the police station when she had gone off on her flight of fantasy.

'I wasn't going anywhere near the island!'

'Take care anyway,' she said. 'Call me if you need anything.'

They had exchanged phone numbers the day before while making their plans for the trip to the police station. She didn't think he would call. After today he must think she was rapidly heading for a mental health crisis.

But he gave her a kind of wave as she drove off, so maybe it wasn't as bad as she imagined.

The day only got worse when Pamela arrived home only a few moments later.

She was getting out of the car on her drive when somebody came out of the house next-door. It wasn't the chief inspector's house, fortunately – that would have been the icing on the cake – but she hadn't met the occupants until now. It was an elderly woman who strode up to her, holding out a hand in welcome.

'Hello – I'm Iris Goodfellow. I'm sorry we haven't come round to introduce ourselves. We've been overseas. My son and his family live in Vancouver.'

'That sounds nice,' said Pamela, discovering that Iris Goodfellow's handshake was rather fearsome.

'It's very mild there, even in the winter,' said Iris. 'Derek won't come out just now – he caught one of his chest infections on the plane.'

After Pamela had expressed her sympathy, Iris got to the point.

'I wouldn't have bothered you when you were just back, only we saw something a wee bit worrying and I thought I'd better let you know at once.'

'Oh, dear,' said Pamela. What on earth could the problem be? She hoped it wasn't anything to do with the dogs making too much noise.

'I was looking out of the kitchen window – the squirrels, you know – and I saw a man climbing over our back wall. There's a rock you can stand on at the far side and that makes it easy to get up. I've tried to get Derek to do something but he says it's too heavy for him and the Council won't do it… Anyway, I was all set to go out and chase him away when he hared across out garden and over into yours. I opened the back door to shout, and I could just see him through that gap in the fence. He was actually at your door and then he looked in at your kitchen window. Well, of course I shouted at him and Derek heard me and came out too, although he shouldn't have been out in the cold and I hope it won't do his chest any harm… Where was I?'

'You shouted at this man in the garden,' Pamela prompted.

'Yes, and he ran down to the far end of your garden and hopped over the wall there, so at least we'd scared him off. I was hoping Mr Mitchell would be in – did you know he's in the police? – such a comfort having him so close by – but he must have been at work. His car had gone, and we tried the door anyway, but there was no answer, of course.'

'Thank you for trying,' said Pamela politely. 'I hope your husband's back in the warm now.'

'Well, we've all got to stick together, haven't we?' said Iris. 'Otherwise it'll be mob rule, and then where will we be?'

Pamela couldn't think of any possible answer to this, but Iris had already shown herself to be the kind of person who was ready to fill a gap that sprang up in any conversation.

'We saw you going out with your wee dogs, by the way. So cute! What are they called?'

'Tiger and Lily,' Pamela muttered.

Iris laughed. 'I must tell Derek. He'll be tickled by that. And don't worry about the noise. We haven't heard a thing yet. And we're used to dogs anyway. Our Katie has one too... Mind you, it probably helps that we're a bit hard of hearing.'

After apologising at length a few more times for keeping Pamela standing in the cold, Iris returned to her house, stepping lithely over a border of rose bushes on the way. An elderly man waved at Pamela from a window. Pamela waved back.

Maybe there was some way of devising an escape route that didn't go past any of their windows. But she'd have to stash the car somewhere else in that case.

Tiger greeted her as if she'd been away for days instead of only an hour, and Lily ignored her for all of five minutes, only to come and sit on her feet in the studio soon afterwards as an apparent gesture of forgiveness. Well, Pamela thought, at least she'd save a bit on heating costs now that she had the dogs to keep her warm.

She glanced out of the studio window, hoping not to see any mysterious strangers outside. She could do without any more of them. She thought uneasily of the man who had tried to steal Tiger. Why on earth would he do that anyway? Yorkshire terriers weren't exactly designer dogs, and Tiger and Lily were among the scruffier examples she had seen of the breed. Unless he had imagined somebody might pay a ransom for them. She supposed she might have done so, if it came to the crunch, but what had even made anybody think that was an option?

She didn't get very far with her commission, because she was still worrying over the intruder and the dog-napper and wondering if they were one and the same man when the door-bell rang.

'Not again!' she muttered to herself. She closed the door of the studio as she went out to the hall. The last thing that would help at this moment would be for her to trip over one of the animals and end up in hospital.

Detective Chief Inspector Mitchell was on the front door-step, and he didn't seem at all happy.

'May I come in for a minute, Mrs Prendergast?' he growled.

She held the door open wide for him.

'We'd better sit in the front room. Don't worry, the dogs aren't there.'

They had hardly had time to sit down before he snapped,

'What do you think you and the Hutchison boy are up to?'

Pamela tried to make her eyes wide and innocent, but she had a feeling it wasn't working.

'The Hutchison boy?'

'I'm not playing games here. Why were you along at the station with him?'

'I said I'd go with him to let the team know he'd got a description of the car that killed his mother. I was only there to give him a bit of confidence.'

'Confidence! Ha!'

'I don't understand why you're being so hostile. I thought you might appreciate some help.'

'We don't need people interfering with witnesses.'

'We weren't – he wasn't. He was just casually chatting to the woman, as far as I know, and she came out with it without being asked. I expect she was wondering why the police hadn't asked her the question. Why hadn't they?'

His eyes narrowed. 'You've got very strong opinions for somebody who has nothing to do with the case. What's your connection with the boy?'

'The dogs,' said Pamela. 'That's the connection.'

She told him about how the dogs had come into her possession. He listened carefully, his expression giving nothing away.

'So how did you know Joanne Hutchison again?' he asked abruptly once she'd finished speaking.

'I didn't.'

'You weren't her social worker or something?'

Pamela didn't know whether to be more enraged by being mistaken for a social worker or angry on Andy's and his mother's behalf about Mitchell's assumption that they needed one.

'No!' she snapped. 'What makes you think they needed a social worker, anyway?'

He shrugged. 'I just thought – mother left on her own to cope – scope for the boy to get into trouble…'

'There are plenty of single parent families who get along just fine without any outside interference,' said Pamela as calmly as she could manage. 'I don't see why the Hutchisons shouldn't have been able to look after themselves.'

'All right, all right,' said the chief inspector. 'So how did your name get into her address book, then?'

'I really don't know. Maybe somebody gave her my name in case she wanted to get in touch.'

As Pamela spoke, she wondered why a stranger should get in touch, unless they were planning to offer her a commission, of course. Had Joanne Hutchison been in a position to commission illustrations for children's books? Or maybe for a mural in the children's corner of a library? Pamela had worked on a couple of similar projects. She should have asked Andy about his mother's job. She might even have worked in a nursery school or a private nursery.

'Do you know what Mrs Hutchison did for a living?' she asked.

The question evidently took him by surprise.

'I don't know, off the top of my head,' he said. His manner had changed now. He was more interested in what she had to say, less aggressive. Not that he'd ever been scarily aggressive, even at the start when he'd stood on the doorstep. 'I can look it up in the case files. We must have established that... Why do you ask?'

She explained about the illustrations and the murals, and he nodded his understanding.

'Just don't go poking about on your own, now,' he advised as she showed him out. 'This isn't your problem, even if the boy isn't satisfied with what we've done so far. You could try and dissuade him from taking things into his own hands, too, if you see him again. You never know what he might stir up.'

'Yes,' she said. 'The forces of evil. Best not to disturb them.'

'This isn't funny,' he said, and walked off towards his car, which he'd left on the street outside.

'I'm not laughing,' Pamela murmured to herself as she closed the front door.

Chapter 9 Quicksand

Pamela didn't go out much for the next few days. She told herself the dogs could make do with the garden – where she always supervised them, using the opportunity to do a bit of tidying up while she was out there – and that all this ferrying them around was playing havoc with her work schedule. In reality, of course, the schedule was non-existent, but she didn't really want to meet anybody and also she still felt uneasy about the man Iris and Derek had seen.

Eventually, though, Tiger became more restless even than usual and she decided she'd have to take them somewhere for a proper run. There had been heavy rain the night before, so the promenade was the obvious choice. She could only begin to imagine how much mud the two of them would trail into the house if she took them to any of the woodland areas.

It was a sense of inevitability that she saw Caitlin French lingering at the foot of the slope near the café. Had the woman been waiting for her? She must have had a long wait in that case.

Caitlin didn't waste any time in pleasantries but rushed up to her and hissed,

'What did you do that for?'

'I don't know what….'

'Setting the police on me again,' said Caitlin, her face too close for comfort. 'Just when I was getting a bit of peace.'

'Setting the police on you?'

'Over Joanne's accident. They were round on Friday, asking questions.'

'What kind of questions?'

'Never mind that! Why did you set them off again?'

'I didn't... Well, we went in to see them last week – maybe that's it,' said Pamela, half to herself. 'But I didn't think they'd taken any notice – and it really didn't have anything to do with you.'

'Ha! Nothing to do with me? That isn't what they thought. Questions about that day – as if I needed reminding about it – about me and Joanne, were we close friends, and did I notice anything about the car, and what about the woman who did first aid? Anybody'd think it was all my fault!'

'Sorry,' said Pamela.

A man came up behind Caitlin and put his arm round her. He glared at Pamela.

'You've set her off again, haven't you?'

'No!' Pamela insisted. 'It wasn't like that.'

'How was it then? Tell me.'

'It was nothing to do with Caitlin. Or anybody. It was just something to do with the car that we thought the police should know.'

He whispered something to Caitlin and she shrugged off his arm, turned and walked away up the slope. Pamela was left facing him on her own. She could hear Tiger growling very softly, while Lily shivered behind her legs.

She refused to let him intimidate her. He wasn't that much taller than she was, his face had an unhealthy pallor and his eyes looked a bit puffy. She told herself she could outrun him if necessary – but what about the dogs? She wouldn't get far if they were under her feet, and by the time she paused to pick up Lily, he could do some serious damage.

'I didn't know they were going to bother Caitlin,' she said in a low voice. 'I know none of it was her fault.'

'Just be careful,' he growled. 'Maybe it was an honest mistake this time, but we'll know if it happens again. Wouldn't want anything to happen to you – or to the dogs.'

It didn't make sense. What would they know? Did he mean that he and Caitlin would know, or were there others involved?

'Are you all right there?' said a different voice.

Pamela had been looking down anxiously at the dogs and hadn't noticed another man approach them. He was young and had on an apron, and she thought she recognised him from the café. She let herself relax a little.

'I was just on my way in for a coffee,' she told him.

'I'll bring something out to you if you want to get a table outside with the dogs,' he said. 'Cappuccino, is it?'

She nodded, so grateful to him that she couldn't speak.

Caitlin's friend turned on his heel and went up the slope. She hoped he wouldn't lurk there and intercept her when she returned to the car, but she would cross that bridge when she came to it.

'You don't want to have anything to do with the likes of them,' said the waiter when he brought out the cappuccino.

'I think I'd worked that out myself, thanks,' she said with a laugh.

He grinned back, but said, rather seriously, 'Maybe you should find somebody to walk with. For a while, anyway.'

'Good idea,' said Pamela, although she wasn't very taken with it. She liked to think while she walked, and she couldn't imagine being able to do that if she had to bring a companion. What if they turned out to be somebody like Iris?

She didn't walk very far that day at all, partly because she found her legs wouldn't carry her, and then she waited to return to her car until an elderly couple and two young children – almost certainly a family group of grandparents and grandchildren – set off up the path that led towards the road. There was no sign that Caitlin's friend or partner was lying in wait for her, but she didn't want to take that risk.

It was ridiculous to feel like this, she told herself. It was broad daylight, and almost all the other people around were harmless dog-walkers or runners. There was no reason to be looking over her shoulder all the time, expecting to be ambushed. She would make the dogs nervous too if she didn't pull herself together. Lily certainly didn't need to be any twitchier than she already was.

Still, it was good to get home and lock all the doors – and go round afterwards checking that she had locked them – and to remind herself that she had a police officer on one side and a couple of nosy neighbours on the other. Surely at least one of them would hear her scream if it came to the crunch.

Maybe it was time to focus on her work for a while. In theory it should drive out the demons, for what could be more innocuous than the set of illustrations she was working on at present? But when she sat down at her desk, Lily immediately settling on her feet as usual, and even Tiger apparently tired and ready to curl up on a cushion under the window, she found herself drawing something completely different.

After a while she sat back and stared in surprise at what she'd done. There were no anthropomorphic mice or rabbits in little jackets and hats, or any animals at all for that matter. She had sketched the scene of Joanne Hutchison's accident as Caitlin had described it. She considered it for a moment or two, and then decided to do it as a kind of comic strip instead of just one sketch.

The end result wasn't bad. Maybe she could branch out into comics. She had never really considered that option before.

She needed more paper. She scrabbled about in the top drawer of the filing cabinet and came up with the sheet she'd sketched Andy Hutchison on. Once again she had that nagging sense of familiarity. Was it only around the eyes? Or something about his range of expressions?

Her gaze fell on the wedding photograph, which she had flung into the same drawer. Her eyes narrowing, she put the two images side by side and looked from one to the other and back.

It was almost as if there was a family resemblance there.

She considered families. The detective chief inspector asking if she had been Joanne Hutchison's social worker. Did he know something more about that particular family? Where was Andy's father? Did he come into the picture at all?

She and Paul hadn't had any children. At first they had wanted to be footloose and fancy-free for a bit longer, and then later they had found it was too late. That must have been a factor in his desire to live on his own during the week, and also in her own failure to talk him out of it. She had known they would probably drift apart, and yet she had done nothing to prevent that, except for encouraging him to come home at weekends, of course. That had given their relationship at least the semblance of stability.

She had the feeling she was about to step from firm ground on to quicksand. Was it a step she was ready to take? Wouldn't it be better to carry on pretending things were exactly as she had imagined them to be than to face up to a reality she had always been able to ignore up to now? But maybe it was the firm ground that was illusory, and the quicksand that would turn out to be real after all. Or that she would have to make her way through the quicksand, difficult though that might be, to reach the place where she needed to be. At that point she realised she had reached for the wrong metaphor. If the next step were indeed to take her into quicksand, she would sink without trace. The next step must be across a river with stepping-stones, or wading through shallow water in which although it was cold and unpleasant, she probably wouldn't drown.

Pamela started to laugh aloud at herself, causing Tiger to jump up from the cushion and break into frantic yapping. Honestly, before she knew where she was she would have left the anthropomorphic rabbits far behind and she'd have embarked on a different journey, one in which trees twisted into horrid shapes lined a dim path into the depths of a dark ravine from which nobody emerged alive. That wasn't her thing at all. Even if she did appear to be on an impossible quest at the moment.

Chapter 10 Maisie and more

After the previous day's experiences, Pamela resolved not to take the dogs down to the Silverknowes promenade until she could persuade somebody else to go with her. She wondered if she might be able to recruit Kim for this purpose, although her friend had never been all that keen on dogs, or on walking for that matter. Or maybe Iris from next-door would agree to come with her. For all Pamela knew, the woman was desperate to get away from Derek for a while. That could be why she had spent so long chatting the other day. Still, she knew almost nothing about the couple, and she told herself not to make assumptions.

It had rained again overnight, which made the woods less attractive, so she decided it wouldn't do the dogs any harm if they just walked round to the cluster of shops where she'd bought the pastries for Kim's visit. It would mean having to skirt the golf course and walk on pavements, which was rather annoying, but she didn't think the golfers would welcome two small dogs on to their territory. But Pamela knew there were gardens at Lauriston Castle, though she hadn't yet explored them, and a park at Davidson's Mains if they even got that far.

The lure of pastries kept her going despite Lily's best efforts to drag her back home almost as soon as they set off. By contrast Tiger looked as if he could walk for hours on end and still have enough energy to worry the cushions on Pamela's favourite chair.

The bakery owner had optimistically placed a table and a couple of chairs out on the pavement, and coffee and warm scones were on offer, so Pamela asked whether the dogs would be in the way if she sat outside with them. She was reluctant after all that had happened to leave them tied up anywhere, even for the time it would take her to drink a cup of coffee. The sun had come out and sitting there was very pleasant.

The woman brought out a dish of water and set it down in front of Tiger. Lily had wedged herself in between Pamela's legs and the wall of the building, just as might have been expected.

'Cute wee dogs. Yorkies, are they?'

'Yes, that's right.'

'I haven't seen them about before.'

'I've only just moved here – well, to Cramond. Pamela Prendergast.'

There was really no need to introduce herself, but the woman had a friendly face, and Pamela felt she could do with all the friends she could get.

'I'm Maisie Macdonald. I hope your dogs don't mind the shop sign.'

Pamela glanced up and noticed the lettering above the door and window for the first time. The Calico Cat! She laughed.

'Great name. Are you a cat-lover, then?'

'I'm afraid so. Maybe you didn't notice the other time you were in here, but I do cat ornaments and so on. In the bit at the back, behind the bakery and the café. If you have any friends who like cats, you should have a look some time in case you see anything they might fancy.'

'I do sometimes draw cats,' said Pamela. 'That's my job, actually – illustrating children's books, and sometimes painting murals for libraries. They often want animals.'

'How very interesting!' exclaimed Maise. 'I've sometimes thought of getting somebody to paint a cat mural in that part of the shop.'

'You should think about it a bit more before deciding,' said Pamela. 'It'd be quite a big project.'

'Yes, that's why I haven't had it done yet,' said Maisie.

A couple of other customers wandered into the shop, and she followed them, so there was no chance for further conversation, but just before Pamela left Maisie returned and asked for her contact details.

'Oh! I wasn't trying to sell my services,' said Pamela, embarrassed.

'Well, maybe you should!' said Maisie reprovingly. 'You never know where you might find a customer. Do you have a business card? Or even just a phone number?'

Still blushing, Pamela fished a slightly crumpled card out of her pocket.

'Sorry, I think this is the only one I have at the moment. That reminds me, I must order another batch.'

'If you had fliers or maybe a poster I could display them in the shop for you,' Maisie offered.

Pamela smiled. 'If I ever need a marketing expert I'll be sure to hire you for the job... You're right, though. I'll organise fliers and a poster once I'm a bit more settled.'

'I like to support local people,' said Maisie. She put the card in the pocket of her apron. 'I'll think about the mural again and let you know.'

'Good,' said Pamela.

It was refreshing to start the day with such a positive encounter. Even if things went downhill from there.

They were passing the entrance to Lauriston Castle on the way home when her mobile phone rang. She was tempted to ignore the call, convinced that nothing good would come of it, but she told herself not to be silly. It might even be one of her publishing contacts offering her a new commission. She couldn't really afford to ignore a call like that.

'Hello? Mrs Prendergast?'

Andy was breathless and panicky.

'Andy?'

'Can I come round and see you?'

'All right. But I'm out with the dogs. We've just got to Lauriston Castle on our way back. Do you want to meet me somewhere?'

'Will you wait for me in the Castle gardens? I won't be long.'

He rang off abruptly. Pamela decided she had no alternative – she changed direction at once and entered the grounds. She hadn't known whether dogs were allowed there or not, but it seemed they were, for she almost collided with a woman who was trying to control some kind of collie, and she could see a couple of golden retrievers in the distance.

Some of the minor paths were enticing, but she decided to stick to the main drive to make sure Andy could find her easily. It had sounded as if he was in a tearing hurry.

Sure enough, he came up behind her at a run only five or ten minutes later, chest heaving and gasping for breath. The dogs set up a clamour, of course, and he had to spend some time greeting them.

'Hadn't you better sit down?' said Pamela, glancing round to see if she could locate a bench or even a rock or fallen tree-trunk where he could perch until he got his breath back.

'I'm – fine,' he said. 'But we need to get out of here. They're after me.'

'Who do you think is after you?'

'I can't explain now... Have you got your car somewhere?'

'It's at home.'

He groaned, and his shoulders slumped. 'How're we going to get out of here without them seeing?'

'It would help if I knew who they were,' said Pamela, trying to keep her temper under control and only just succeeding. She knew her tone could probably have competed with the most censorious of school teachers. 'Are you sure they saw you coming in here?'

'Even if they didn't, they'll look here – it's obvious. They nearly caught me at that roundabout by the golf course.'

'Maybe we could hide somewhere in the gardens,' Pamela suggested.

It was a silly idea, of course. The last thing she wanted to do with the rest of the morning was to play hide and seek with Andy and whoever it was who had frightened him out of his wits. Unfortunately he seized on it and began looking wildly round for possible hiding-places.

'What about the dogs?' she said. 'They're bound to make a noise.'

'You don't need to hide,' he told her. 'You and the dogs can start a diversion – get the gardeners or somebody to come after you. I'll do the hiding part.'

This was getting worse and worse.

'All right – find somewhere to hide. If I let Tiger off the lead, you'll have to help me catch him, though.'

'Don't let him off the lead. He'll lead them straight to me.'

These were his final words before he plunged into the nearest shrubbery. He had only just disappeared from view when two men ran up the drive. Tiger and Lily started barking again, even more frantically than before.

One of the men recognised either Pamela or the dogs straight away, and she recognised him too. It was Caitlin's friend or partner, the one who had already threatened her once. She prepared to scream or fight, or both. But just as they drew level with her, two women appeared at her side, one of them towed along by a ferocious-looking animal almost the size of a small pony. Pamela tried to draw the Yorkies out of its reach, but the woman who wasn't holding the lead said blithely,

'Don't you worry, he's already had his main meal of the day.'

Under other circumstances Pamela would have taken to her heels and scurried away from the two of them and the ugly beast they were in charge of, but for now she was content to stay and chat to them. The two men had already come to a halt a few metres away, and looked as if they were debating with each other what to do next. After a few minutes they turned and walked away. Would they wait round the next corner to mount their attack? She doubted whether they'd given up altogether, though with luck she and Andy could evade their clutches for today.

They had no transport to hand, but Pamela had the number of a taxi firm stored in her phone, and even now, long after her mother's death and after most transactions were now carried out by contactless card, she still tended to carry enough cash in her purse to get her home in an emergency.

The taxi came right into the Castle grounds for them. Andy was reluctant to get in at first, saying he had to get back to wherever it was he lived now, but she overrode his objections, and only minutes later they were getting out at the bungalow. Even there he shielded his face as he walked up the short drive to the front door.

It was clear the chase had completely unnerved him. She didn't have much experience of young men of his age, but generally the ones she had encountered were not easily rattled. But then, she would have thought of herself as rather unflappable, and yet when it came to the crunch she'd turned out not to be.

She was relieved to be able to unclip the dogs' leads and let them run on ahead to the kitchen looking for food. Andy hung back, watching as she fed them and re-filled their water dish.

'Would you like something to eat too?' she asked him. 'I'm only going to make a sandwich now, but there's fruit cake in the cupboard.'

By the time she had put a snack lunch on the kitchen table, he had thawed enough to take his seat opposite her and to demolish the cheese and tomato sandwiches and drain a mug of coffee, and she had come up with a wild idea. She wasn't sure how he would take it, but it was worth a try, and she hoped it would help her too.

Chapter 11 Revelations

'No, I'd better be getting back,' said Andy.

'What if they come after you again, though?' asked Pamela.

He shrugged. 'It'll be fine.'

It wasn't going to be fine, and they both knew it. Something was badly wrong.

'Please, just stay here. It's only for a while, until we can straighten it all out.... Maybe the police...'

'The police won't do anything. They're not interested.'

'They might get interested, if we can work out what it's about.'

He gave her an amused, somewhat scornful look. 'How are we meant to do that, then?'

'Well, just stay for tonight, then. Maybe they'll have forgotten about you by tomorrow.'

That seemed highly unlikely, but Pamela was rather reluctant to let him out of her sight. She wasn't sure why she should suddenly feel responsible for him, even if he did seem to be all alone in the world. He wasn't her problem. Paul would have told her that in so many words, if he'd been here. Suddenly she wished he could be here, for even if they had lived parts of their lives separately, she'd always known there was somebody on her side.

Or maybe that had been an illusion. After all, she hadn't known about the studio. That reminded her that the lawyers hadn't got back to her about the Glasgow side of things. Maybe she should chase them up. But even thinking about it made her feel very tired.

'I can make up the sofa-bed easily enough,' she said. 'It's in my studio, so I'm afraid nothing's very tidy… Would you like to see the studio?'

He wouldn't be interested in her work, of course – it was too cute to appeal to a teenage boy – but maybe he'd like to do some sketching of his own.

To her surprise, his face lit up with enthusiasm.

'That'd be good. I'm doing art at college – as well as all the boring stuff.'

'Boring stuff?'

'Just the usual things, maths, English, physics, geography. Mum wanted me to go in for science.'

They went through to the studio. She closed the door behind them, shutting out the dogs. With luck they were too tired to scratch the door down, at least not for a little while.

'Were you thinking of making a career of it? Art, I mean?'

'Too soon to say,' he said, but his tone was wistful, as if he had already resigned himself to stacking shelves or answering phones for his entire working life.

'My Dad was an artist,' he added as they approached Pamela's desk.

'Really? I mean, that's interesting.'

'Well, a designer really. He – what's that?'

Andy was staring down at the desk as if mesmerised.

Pamela realised she'd left the wedding photo lying about, and the sketch of Andy himself was under it. Would he think she was a bit weird, drawing a portrait of somebody she hardly knew? But he had picked up the photo and ignored the sketch.

His face went white, and she was afraid he might keel over, so she pushed him gently into her work chair. He had a death-grip on the photo. She wanted to take it away from him but it might tear if she did so, and she had a kind of sentimental feeling that she needed to keep it, as Paul had kept it by him throughout the years of partial separation. Or at least until he moved to a new studio without even telling her.

'It's my wedding photo,' she said calmly, although her anger over Paul's secrecy had resurfaced and was threatening to overcome every other emotion.

It wasn't Andy's fault, she told herself. Whatever had happened between Paul and herself, the teenager could not possibly be held responsible.

'It's my Dad,' he replied a moment later.

'No – that's Paul. Paul Prendergast. My late husband.'

Maybe if she told herself often enough, she would believe it.

She sat down with a bump on the sofa-bed that stood against the far wall.

'Paul Hutchison,' said Andy stubbornly. 'My father.'

They stared at each other. Andy placed the photo carefully back on the desk and picked up the sketch instead.

'Is this me?'

She nodded silently.

'What did you want to draw me for?'

'I do that sometimes,' said Pamela. 'I sketch people and animals I come across. I can't help it – it's a sort of compulsion. Particularly if I feel a bit upset about something.'

He nodded this time. 'I can understand that... Did you know he was my Dad?'

She must be honest with him. 'When I looked at my sketch of you, I thought I saw a resemblance, but I told myself I was imagining things. I suppose I didn't want to think about the implications.'

'Is that why...?'

'Why I helped you today? Why I asked you to stay? Not really – I just knew you were in trouble, and I didn't want to have whatever might happen to you next on my conscience.'

He fell silent again, and placed the drawing on the desk top, next to the photo. He glanced between the two images.

'You are quite like him,' said Pamela. 'Round the eyes, mostly.'

'He's dead, then.'

'What?'

'You said he was your late husband.'

'Didn't you know?'

He shook his head.

'He drowned crossing the causeway to Cramond Island when the tide was coming in,' said Pamela. There was no point in trying to hide the basic facts from Andy now. 'They're still deciding on whether to hold a fatal accident inquiry.'

Andy blinked once or twice, then got up from the chair and stumbled over to the window, where he gripped the sill and stood there staring at the garden for some time. It was no use offering comfort, either in words or gestures. He wouldn't want that from her, not yet anyway. But she would have to keep him here. There was no way he should be alone, certainly not tonight.

By the time he turned back towards her, he was outwardly calm. She remembered the numbness that had come over her when she'd first heard the news of Paul's death from the police. With luck, Andy would experience something similar. She had thought at the time, with the other part of her mind that still kept her functioning more or less normally, that it was nature's way of protecting her from being completely overwhelmed by death. But maybe her mind worked differently from his in that respect. She'd had more time to build up inner resilience than he had. Was that the secret to it?

At least he wasn't distraught. She wouldn't have had a clue what to do if grief had made him violent, either towards her or himself, though she supposed at least that would have given her some valid reason to call on her neighbour to help.

'We didn't know,' he said. 'Mum thought he'd just – vanished. He'd sent us away on holiday for a week. At Blackpool. We saw the lights. He said he had to spend the week with his mother. He didn't come home again after that… I could tell she'd started to think he'd never come back, but she didn't say anything, and then there was the accident.'

'But didn't she report him missing, or something?'

He shrugged. 'She didn't say anything to me about it. Maybe she didn't want to worry me at the time. I was in the middle of my first term assignments. When he hadn't come home by Christmas I asked her where he was. She said his mother was terminally ill and he'd gone to stay with her again… I kind of thought maybe he was in touch with her by phone or text while he was away, but from what you're saying, he couldn't have been.'

'Paul usually came home at weekends,' said Pamela, although she did wonder whether 'home' was the right word for it. He might have felt more at home with Joanne and Andy, for all she knew. Or maybe he had just wanted the best of both worlds. 'To our flat, I mean. The one in the New Town,' she added as if he might not remember bringing the dogs there.

'Home' said Andy. He sat down at the desk again, flopping into it as if his legs wouldn't hold him upright any longer. 'He said he had to be with his mother and sister at weekends. He said his sister was disabled and his Mum needed him more than we did. But he was with you all the time.'

'Well, I thought he was in his flat in Glasgow during the week!' said Pamela indignantly, thinking she heard an accusing note in his voice.

'We did live in Glasgow until not long ago,' said Andy slowly. 'Then we moved here. I never knew why at the time. I hated changing schools – that's why I'm doing my Highers at the college instead.' He glanced across at her. 'He made it all up, about his disabled sister and his Mum, didn't he? And then my Mum made up the part about terminal illness after she decided he wasn't coming back.'

She nodded. 'His mother died years ago, and I never heard of a sister.'

He put both hands on the desk and stared at them with apparent loathing. 'Why didn't she tell me instead of making up more stories? Was she covering up his double life all along?'

Pamela tried to think of something positive to say about Andy's father.

'He was a really good jewellery designer. One of the best,' she added. 'I don't suppose he set out to lie to all of us. It probably just happened… We didn't have huge arguments or anything, so he must've still thought of us as married. We did live mostly separate lives for a long time. And we couldn't have children together. Paul and your Mum and you were more of a family.'

'How did he do it, though?'

Andy sounded resigned rather than angry. Maybe the anger would surface later.

'He must have had to work it out really carefully,' said Pamela. 'If he was calling himself Paul Hutchison, maybe he had a whole separate identity – officially, I mean. Another national insurance number, another birth certificate, the whole works. And he swapped them all over when he came to the flat for the weekend. The police would've come to see your Mum after he died if they'd found any sign of his Hutchison identity on him. That's what happens when somebody dies in suspicious circumstances – they unearth all the guilty secrets.'

'But if you didn't suspect it, then they wouldn't either,' said Andy slowly. 'There was no thread to pull on that would've unravelled the whole thing.'

'The only connection between his two identities was my name in your Mum's address book,' said Pamela. 'I wonder how that happened.'

'It was in his writing,' said Andy. 'With a scribble at the side saying it was for emergencies, or something like that.'

'It's a pity he didn't do the same thing for me. Though he'd have had trouble explaining it.'

'It's kind of weird, though, isn't it?' said Andy. 'I mean – them both dying in accidents. What are the chances?'

'You're right, it's too much of coincidence.'

'We need to find out more,' said Andy.

Pamela shivered. 'Do we really?'

'Well, somebody has to. It obviously isn't finished yet.'

She thought of Caitlin's friend, and the dog-napper, and the man in her garden. Then there were Andy's pursuers today. He was right. They wanted something – was it revenge for something Paul or Joanne had done? Or had Paul been involved in other, even dodgier activities as well as his dual identities? Maybe he'd fallen foul of some criminal gang who had chased him out of Glasgow and tracked him down here.

There were all sorts of scary possibilities. Pamela was certain she hadn't even scratched the surface of her imagination. Even the move from the New Town to Cramond, at Paul's instigation, seemed suspicious now. And what if she had bumped into the Hutchison family somewhere locally? It must surely have increased the risk of him being found out in his deception. And the result had been to bring danger to all of them. For a moment Pamela fervently wished that she'd been able somehow to stop the sale of the flat and to stay there, with the centuries-old solidity of grey stone all around and at least one or two neighbours she'd been acquainted with, though she couldn't say they were exactly friends.

But, as the lawyers had explained to her, the sale of the flat and the purchase of this bungalow had gone too far by the time of Paul's death to be easily halted, and she hadn't had the mental energy at the time to look at alternatives, so here she was.

One of the dogs scratched at the door suddenly, interrupting her train of thought, such as it was.

'Will I let them in?' she asked Andy.

'If you want.'

Both dogs scampered in and made a huge fuss of both Pamela and Andy, as if they'd been parted for days. Paul must have liked dogs after all. He'd never given her any indication of it, in all the years they'd been married. Or maybe he just put up with them for Joanne's sake.

'Dad got the dogs when we moved here,' said Andy, destroying that thought before it was even properly formed. 'He thought Mum needed a bit of company – she only worked mornings, so she was in the house a lot.'

'Did she walk them along the promenade?' asked Pamela, more for something to say than because she wanted to know.

He nodded. 'I think that's where she knew Caitlin from.'

It wasn't the right time to ask Andy if he'd met Caitlin's partner, or whether he had recognised him during that day's chase.

It wasn't the right time to speculate aloud about possible connections between the two deaths, even if Andy had started it.

What they needed was something to eat. And a good night's sleep.

Pamela didn't think she could guarantee a good night's sleep for either of them, but one thing she could do was to order a pizza. Or alternative cuisine of Andy's own choice.

Chapter 12 Assembling the Pieces

In the morning, Andy made noises about going back to his bedsit to get changed. After having to leave the house where he and his mother – and Paul – had lived, he'd managed to find a place with the help of the college authorities, and he seemed to have landed on his feet with a motherly landlady who fed him well. All the same, Pamela was reluctant to let him leave her house yet. She wouldn't have been able to live with herself if his pursuers of the previous day had caught up with him. And there were more mysteries for the two of them to tease out, too.

She remembered having to bring a box of Paul's things with her from the flat – she'd meant to dispose of everything before the move, with the idea of a fresh start where she wouldn't be haunted by memories, but in the event there just hadn't been time to sort through it all. Some of his clothes had been almost new, not surprisingly since he'd only been there at weekends to wear them, and she had taken them to charity shops. Had he had a completely separate wardrobe for his life as Paul Hutchison? Where did he change over in that case. She imagined him going into a phone box somewhere between Glasgow and Edinburgh, or more recently between Silverknowes and the New Town, and coming out as somebody quite different. The mental image made her laugh inappropriately just as she was opening the box of clothes.

He'd have been lucky to find a proper phone box between Silverknowes and the New Town these days, even for a superhero emergency.

She suppressed another giggle.

'What's so funny?' said Andy, materialising just at her shoulder in the room that she had meant to use as a dining-room but which was literally a box-room for now. He peered into the open box. 'What's in there?'

'Some of Paul's things,' she said, her mirth evaporating instantly. 'I thought there might be something you could wear. Just for now, I mean. Until you can get back home and change.'

He made a derisive sound. 'I wouldn't be seen dead – I mean, sorry. I can't wear his things. It wouldn't be right.'

'Maybe a sweatshirt or something?'

She pulled out a top in rugby colours. Maybe not.

She tipped the box up and let the rest of the contents spill out across the wood-effect laminate floor. Something clattered when it fell. A watch? A phone? Pamela frowned. Paul's phone had been found on his person, ruined by the salt water of course.

She rummaged among the random items of clothing to find the thing that had made the noise, and came up with a small leather bag. It was in the style of an ancient coin purse that might have held medieval coins or other treasure, with a drawstring at the top. What was it, and how had it ended up in this box? Her fingers fumbled when she tried to loosen the string.

'What is it?' said Andy.

She gave it to him. 'Can you open it? My fingers are too clumsy.'

Her fingers were trembling, of course. With anticipation, even dread.

Andy opened it easily, and poured the contents out on to one of the striped shirts Paul had worn a decade or so earlier and then discarded.

They gasped in unison.

Pamela sat back on her heels and closed her eyes. Of course there had to be jewels somewhere in the mix. She should have known.

'Are they real?' said Andy, wide-eyed. He prodded at one of the more colourful stones.

'I don't know,' said Pamela. Her feeling of dread had intensified dramatically. She opened her eyes and stared at the floor. 'He never brought home anything he was working on,' she said. 'He always said the insurance wouldn't cover it. I hardly ever saw any of it, except when he sent me pictures.'

How had they got into the box of things from the New Town flat? That thought sparked another one.

'The box from his studio!' she exclaimed. 'I've only looked at the top layer. I got – distracted – by the wedding photo.'

'From his studio?' said Andy. 'How did it get here? They wouldn't have known…'

'It was from his old studio,' she said, suddenly weary. 'His first one. In Glasgow. They said he'd moved on from there and left some things behind. Including the wedding photo, of course. Why would he hang on to that if he was creating a new identity?'

'I went to his Glasgow studio once, when I was wee,' said Andy. 'About six or seven. I was still at primary school, anyway. He showed me how he made the settings. And he gave me a book of his designs. I've still got that… He wouldn't let me go there again, though. Mum said he didn't want me getting in his way. But I wouldn't have done. I would've liked just to watch him.'

'He liked to work on his own,' said Pamela. 'He said it was cheaper to run a studio in Glasgow, but of course it wasn't really. He just made that up to put some distance between us. I can see that now. Of course it's only since I met you that I've known why.'

He flinched.

'It isn't your fault,' Pamela added. 'Or your Mum's fault. She wasn't to know... Wait there.'

She fetched the box that had been sent over from the Glasgow studio, and placed it on the floor between them. If there were any surprises inside, Andy deserved to know as soon as she did. But she didn't quite have the same sense of dread about this one. Paul wouldn't have left anything behind in that first studio unless it no longer meant anything to him.

She took the items out one by one and arranged them round her on what was left of the floor space. An irregular lump of metal – maybe something he'd used to practise on. Some coloured glass gems that were obviously not worth anything. A sketchbook. She passed that on to Andy, who might like to have it to go with the other book he'd mentioned. A bundle of loose papers. She leafed through them – mostly bills, by the look of it. Was that the reason for moving out of the original studio? Had he been pursued by creditors? That would have been depressing and sordid, and also rather unlikely since Pamela would have paid the bills for him in those days if she'd known about them.. Still, maybe he'd been ashamed of himself – also unlikely – and hadn't wanted to ask her.

It was all water under the bridge now, in any case.

Andy was still occupied with the sketchbook.

'Those are really good,' he said, glancing up for a moment. 'Must have been before he got commercial.'

Pamela hadn't thought of Paul's success in those terms. Of course, Andy was of a different generation, or just in a much younger age-group. She and Paul had both been ridiculously averse at first to doing anything that might make them some money. Andy probably saw her own art as a compromise too.

'What kind of area do you think you'll specialise in?' she asked him suddenly. 'Or is it too soon to say?'

She supposed it was too soon. He might still change his mind altogether about what he wanted to do for a living.

'I like sculpture,' he said. 'But I don't know if I'll be good enough. I probably won't know until I've been studying it for years.'

'But you'd like to go to art college?'

He nodded. 'If I get the grades. And have a good enough portfolio… I won't know that until I try.'

'What did your mum do?'

'You mean for a living?'

Pamela nodded.

'She worked in the office at a nursery. Just part-time though, in the mornings. She couldn't get any more hours. She did try, after my Dad – disappeared. She didn't know if we'd be able to keep the house, even then.'

The house in Silverknowes must have been rented, Pamela realised. She was surprised Paul hadn't bought them somewhere to live. After all, he had had the Glasgow flat to sell. He could have taken out life insurance to cover the mortgage and then Joanne and

Andy would have been all right. Though not, of course, if they hadn't known he was dead.

He had left them in a very awkward situation, she realised suddenly. Not knowing what had happened to him was even worse than knowing. Joanne must have imagined all sorts of things – that he had simply walked out on them, or that he'd had an accident and lost his memory. Because he'd lived with them under a fake identity, they wouldn't have heard about his death even if somebody mentioned it casually.

Though wouldn't they have been a bit suspicious if anybody had said something about a man called Paul who had died on Cramond causeway? Joanne had had Pamela's name and address, too. Why hadn't she got in touch then?

The remains of Paul's life were all around them now. It wasn't all that much to show for the man he'd been.

'Did he have his own studio when you moved to Silverknowes?' she asked Andy.

He glanced up from the page he was staring at.

'He had a shed in the garden. He called it his studio. He'd got permission from the landlord to do some of his work in there.'

'What did you do with the things he'd left in there?'

'Oh, the shed caught fire, so there wasn't anything left,' said Andy casually. 'The landlord wasn't all that pleased, but there was nothing he could do. It was all gone.'

'Caught fire? When did that happen? Was it before Paul – your Dad – disappeared, or after?'

'After,' said Andy. 'Not long before Mum's accident. She was quite cross. Said it must've been vandals. Said I shouldn't go around with them.... I wasn't, though. Not by then.. It was funny, mind you. I thought she'd done it herself. But I don't think she had.'

Pamela blinked. She was surprised he didn't get more upset as he told her this, but she supposed having lost both father and mother within a relatively short space of time, he didn't have much emotion left over to mourn the loss of a garden shed.

He glanced over at her. 'I was quite angry with both of them – him for going away, and her for getting herself run over. Too angry to feel sad about anything. And I had to try and concentrate on getting through my exams, and making sure the dogs were all right.'

Pamela had forgotten about the dogs. She sincerely hoped they were still all right in the kitchen and hadn't found anything to eat that they shouldn't. Chocolate was bad for dogs, wasn't it? There must be other foods that were too. Had she left anything lying about? And it must be past the usual time for their walk too. She scrambled to her feet.

'The dogs – I should walk them before it gets any later. Or maybe I'll just take them round the garden for once. They're not really used to it yet, and I need to see if they find any more holes in the fence or anything.'

He laughed. 'Tiger was always getting out. There were woods behind our house though, so it was all right. Mum didn't like it though. She worried he might get on to the main road.'

'He seemed to like the Chief Inspector's garden,' said Pamela. 'You'd better stay in the house.

Mr Mitchell might see you and start wondering... He's already warned me off poking my nose into – well, your Mum's accident, for one thing.'

'Well, somebody has to,' said Andy. 'The police didn't seem too bothered.'

The dogs were lively, although no more lively than Pamela's thoughts, which scampered through her mind at a great rate, but didn't seem inclined to escape from it, instead retracing their route time and again.

There were no further escapes, though Tiger spent some time snuffling about at the side gate. She tried not to imagine he had detected the scent of an intruder. It was very much more likely to have been a cat or even a fox. She hadn't considered before that there might be foxes around here. That was just another thing to worry about, though it would probably be submerged under all the other things before long. She glanced over at DCI Mitchell's house, and almost decided to tell him the whole story. But apart from the fact that he was probably out investigating something far more important, he wouldn't have time to listen to some half-baked story about fake identities, fake jewels and the whole fake life Paul had invented for himself. It was up to her and Andy to get their ideas in order before they approached the police again.

She was glad to have somebody by her side who understood the situation, even if it was only a teenage boy. Sooner or later he would get distracted and go off and do his own thing. She knew that. But for the moment at least, they were allies.

Chapter 13 Cupboard Love

Just as Pamela brought the dogs back indoors, the front doorbell rang. She could see the outline of a figure through the ornamental glass in the top half of the door. It was a bit late in the day for the postman, although she knew they'd been working odd hours recently.

She left the dogs in the kitchen and went down the hall to open the door.

Iris stood on the door-step, and a grumpy-faced man was waiting behind her.

'Hello, Pamela – I just thought I'd introduce you to Derek, so that you two would know each other. We saw you coming back in a taxi earlier – is there something wrong?'

'Oh no, nothing wrong,' Pamela lied. 'Just that we walked a bit too far and I wasn't sure if the dogs would make it back. They've got such little legs.'

'Of course,' said Iris. 'Such little sweeties,' she added in an oddly flat tone. 'Did you go down to the beach today? Or was it too breezy for you? You wouldn't want the wee dogs to get blown off their feet.'

Was there some kind of threat embedded in the words? Pamela told herself not to imagine things. The round, blonde, immaculately dressed Iris could never threaten anybody.

Her husband Derek was another matter. He loomed behind his wife like a dark cloud waiting to unleash its fury.

Pamela addressed him. 'Quite a nice day for a round of golf, if you're keen on it.'

He gave a soft growl of dissent.

'Oh, Derek doesn't believe in golf,' said Iris. 'A good walk spoiled, that kind of thing. So you didn't go to the beach, then?'

'No – we walked the other way for a while. Towards Lauriston Castle.'

'That's a long walk along pavements. No wonder your wee dogs got worn out.'

'I should really have known better,' said Pamela, trying not to sound apologetic. She thought she had probably failed in that, because Iris gave her an approving smile. 'I'll take the car the next time we go that way. There's a nice café just before you get to the mini-roundabout.'

'Oh, you got that far, did you? No wonder you needed a taxi back. If it happens again, you must give us a call. We're usually at home, aren't we, Derek?'

'Mostly,' he grunted.

'I'll write the number down for you now,' said Iris. 'Do you have a pencil and paper? I usually keep one by the phone.'

Oh yes, you would, thought Pamela. She was starting to develop a strong aversion to Iris, although that seemed unfair when they had exchanged so few words, relatively. They wouldn't exchange many more, if she had her way, and she certainly wouldn't be phoning them, especially if she were in trouble.

She fetched an old envelope and a pen from the shelf in the hall and presented them to the woman.

'Sorry I haven't got anything better to write on just now,' she lied.

'What you need is one of these special message pads,' said Iris after she had written down the number. 'Ask somebody to give you one for Christmas. It's a nice stocking-filler.'

Pamela hadn't been planning to think about Christmas for some time, as it was only April, but she said vaguely, 'That's a good idea. Well, thank you for calling. I'd invite you in for a cup of tea, but I'm afraid I'm all at sixes and sevens. Packing boxes all over the place. We must do that once I get straightened out.'

For a moment Iris looked as if she might barge in regardless, but Derek muttered something and she said instead, 'Of course, dear. Or you can come to us. Just ring the bell any time.'

'I'll do that,' Pamela called after them as they made their way back to their own lair, stepping carefully over the small strip of flower-bed that evidently marked the dividing line between the two small front gardens. 'When hell freezes over,' she added to herself in a whisper once she heard their front door click shut.

There was definitely something about Iris and Derek that brought out the worst in her.

Andy was still where she had left him, sitting on the floor surrounded by what was left of his father's life.

'I like his drawings,' he said, holding up the sketchbook. 'Maybe he should've stuck to that, instead of going commercial.'

It wasn't the right time to give him the talk about how difficult it was to earn a living from true art, but Pamela felt she had to make some excuse for Paul's choice – and her own, for that matter.

'It's hard to stick to it, unless you can find somebody who's willing to pay for it,' she said.

'You're an artist too, aren't you?'

His tone was almost accusing. Had he woken up in the night and browsed through her work? Or was he remembering that moment when he'd seen the sketch of himself?

'I do children's book illustrations. Sometimes murals – for nurseries. And libraries, if they have a children's corner.'

He nodded.

'I wouldn't have enough to live on if I hadn't managed to get some television work,' she added. She told him the name of the children's series she had worked on, and he laughed.

'I used to watch that one! What's it like, working with tv people?'

'They're much the same as anybody else really,' said Pamela. In truth her part of the work had mostly been done at her desk at home. 'The murals are my favourite. I enjoy the larger scale stuff.'

'Me too,' he said with enthusiasm. 'When it comes to sculpture, I mean. Do you know the Master of the Universe? And the Angel of the North?'

They discussed massive sculptures of their acquaintance for a while, then she remembered Tiger and Lily were in the kitchen and they adjourned there to feed the dogs, and she found herself cooking for him this time.

Unfortunately he seemed to like more or less the same foods as his father had, and because Pamela had reviewed her eating choices when she was preparing to live alone, few of Andy's favourites were available. Still, she managed to cobble together a meal of pasta and ice-cream from the random ingredients in the cupboard and freezer. They were random because they consisted of a few tins she had brought with her from her New Town cupboard, thinking they might come in useful in emergencies such as not being able to find her way to the nearest supermarket after moving house, and basic items she'd bought on the way when she noticed a parking space outside a small shop. Ideally she would have stocked up in a superstore by now, but with so much else going on, such as exercising the dogs and playing host to Andy, food shopping hadn't arrived on her radar yet.

He seemed neutral as far as the pasta was concerned but obviously enjoyed the ice-cream.

'What are we going to do?' he asked suddenly after he'd finished scraping all the residue off the bowl and almost getting rid of the pattern in the process.

'What are we going to do when?' she replied, running hot water into the sink for the washing-up.

'Haven't you got a dishwasher for that?'

'Oh – I suppose I have. It isn't worth putting it on just for me, so I forgot about it.'

'You could let the dishes pile up for days,' he suggested.

'I'd rather wash them as I go along… It's up to you what you want to do next. Haven't you got an exam coming along soon?'

He nodded. 'Geography next week. Then Maths the week after. Brutal.' He shuddered theatrically.

'I can give you a lift to college whenever you like. It'll be easier if you stay here, but I'll understand if you want to get back to your place.'

'I should go back. Mrs Paton's bound to be worrying.'

'Well, let me at least take you back there.'

'I've been out on my own before, you know,' he said, but she sensed he wanted to accept her offer. Did he want her to talk him into staying here? It was hard to tell.

'Maybe you should collect some things and come back here. Just until we can get it all sorted out.'

'That could take a while.'

Again she had the feeling he wanted to accept, but felt uncertain of his ground.

'Well, now that we know about the – family connection – I feel a bit responsible for you. In a weird way.'

'Same with me,' said Andy, and grinned at her. 'You're my stepmother.'

'I am not!'

'All right, an auntie, then. I never had any real ones, but one of Mum's friends made me call her Auntie Freda.'

'Was she a friend here or back in Glasgow?'

'Glasgow. My Mum didn't really keep up with her after that. Or with anybody else.'

'I expect there was too much going on,' said Pamela. It was easier to discuss this kind of thing with him while she was turned away, looking down at the dishes in the sink.

'There was,' he agreed. 'Even before Dad – disappeared. Men used to come to the door asking for him, and Mum had to pretend he wasn't in.'

'Who were they? Debt collectors?'

'Might have been. I don't know – nobody would tell me. They just pretended nothing had happened.'

'Did it worry you, though?' she enquired.

'There was only that one time,' he said thoughtfully. 'When I overheard them talking to Mum. It was like something in a tv show. A protection racket or something. They said to tell Dad he'd had his last chance. I'd forgotten that. It wasn't long before we went on holiday, either… What if they killed him? Or him and then Mum?'

'Paul died in an accident,' said Pamela. She turned away from the washing-up so that she could see his face as she spoke. 'The police didn't even consider whether anybody else might have been involved. He was overtaken by the incoming tide and drowned. The only question in my mind was what he'd been doing there at that time of night. It was only later that I found out there might be an inquiry… Did anybody suggest your Mum's accident was anything but an accident?'

'Not really,' said Andy. 'Except that the driver could be done for dangerous driving if they ever caught him.'

'Of course, the police didn't know about Paul's double life,' said Pamela slowly. 'I wonder if the jewels we found are real. That might make a difference too. They might be worth killing somebody for.'

Andy blinked. He suddenly looked very tired, and very young.

'You'd better get some sleep, if you're going to be ready for your exams,' she told him.

'All right, Auntie Pam, see you in the morning,' he said cheekily, but he trudged off to bed without any argument. Of course he was probably planning to play games on his phone until the early hours, but she wasn't going to start an argument about that.

Chapter 14 Taken

Andy was still cheerful the following morning. He had agreed to collect some more clothes from his room, explain things to the landlady and then come back with Pamela for a few nights to give the people who'd been after him some time to change their minds. She didn't even want to think about what might happen if they didn't.

She might have known the day wouldn't progress in the way they had planned.

The street where Andy lived with Mrs Paton wasn't all that far from Pamela's bungalow. The area was respectable enough, and she was just thinking she could safely leave him there to get on with his life when she turned the corner and noticed a police car parked at the kerb.

'What do they want here?' said Andy, and added almost at once, 'Just drive on past – they're right outside Mrs Paton's!'

But as she pulled out to pass the police car, an officer stepped off the pavement and waved her down. There was nothing else for it but to stop. The dogs started yapping from the back seat. Tiger tried to jump through the gap between the seats but Pamela put out a hand to stop him.

Andy hunched down in the front seat, glowering indiscriminately around.

The officer opened the passenger door.

'Out!'

'Just a minute,' said Pamela.

But the officer didn't even glance at her. Neither did Andy. He didn't get out either, though.

'Andy Hutchison?' said the officer after a very short pause.

Andy nodded.

'You're wanted for questioning. Get out of the car.'

'What's this about?' said Pamela.

The officer did glance her way this time. 'Keep out of this, or we'll take you in as well. And keep the dogs under control while you're at it.'

She wanted to ask him if he'd ever tried to control Yorkshire terriers once they got over-excited, but she didn't want to make things any worse for Andy.

'You'd better go with them,' she advised him, in an undertone.

He gave a heavy sigh, but he undid his seat-belt and got out of the car.

'Where are you taking him?' she asked. She had to raise her voice and repeat the question before the officer replied.

'Are you family?'

'Yes,' she lied. Well, it wasn't exactly a lie. More of a slight distortion of the truth.

He gave her the address of the same police station they'd visited only a day or two before.

'Have you got your phone?' she called to Andy.

He gave a very brief nod, and then he was being hustled away into the police car. It drove off rather fast before she could even get out to close the passenger door, and vanished into the distance.

Pamela didn't know whether it was worth trying to follow them to the police station or not, but in any case that was academic because a large woman came out of the nearest house and intercepted her before she could get back into the driving seat.

'What's all this about?'

'Mrs Paton?'

'Aye, that's me. Who are you?'

'My name's Pamela Prendergast. I'm a kind of distant relative of Andy's. He asked me to help him with something.'

Mrs Paton looked unconvinced. 'He doesn't have any family of his own left.'

The last thing Pamela wanted to do was to explain her relationship to Andy while standing out in the street in an unfamiliar neighbourhood – although maybe it would have been even worse in a familiar one – but she could see Andy's landlady wasn't going to be appeased by generalities.

'It's a bit complicated,' she said. 'I was once married to Andy's father.'

Mrs Paton nodded. 'One of those families, eh?'

'Yes.'

To her surprise, after another appraising look the landlady suddenly smiled and said,

'Just as well he's got somebody of his own, though. Better than being alone in the world... Do you want to come in for a minute and you can tell me a bit more about what's going on here.'

'Well, I really wanted – yes, maybe I'd better do that.'

Pamela realised that getting Mrs Paton on their side would be a good move. She had no illusions about Andy wanting to stay on at the bungalow with her once the danger was over, and he could do worse than live under this woman's roof while he continued at college. They'd passed the college on the way here, and he'd be hard pressed to find accommodation much closer to it.

Maybe Mrs Paton could be an honorary granny or something. It was no sillier than Pamela appointing herself stepmother or auntie.

Over coffee and shortbread, Pamela found herself telling the landlady a bit more than she had intended to. She didn't go into the details of her own relationship with Paul, which was almost impossible to explain to an outsider, and as more information emerged, was becoming rather difficult to explain even to herself, but she explained about Andy's parents having both died in unusual circumstances, and about the men who had been pursuing Andy the previous day.

'He told me about his Mum's accident,' said Mrs Paton, 'but I didn't know his Dad had died in an accident too.'

'It was a while ago – before his Mum died,' said Pamela. She hoped the landlady would assume it had happened a year or more ago and would accept that as a reasonable explanation for Andy's silence on the subject.

She wondered about the police suddenly taking Andy in for questioning. They had seemed hostile, even aggressive, in their manner, as if they suspected him of something. Maybe she and Andy had stirred something up when they'd been to the police station. Not just DCI Mitchell's ire but something more serious. Though surely there was no way he could have been involved in his mother's accidental death. He'd probably been at college at the time, apart from anything else. Pamela suddenly wished she had checked that out with him. She could have done it without appearing to suspect him of anything.

She jumped up from her chair, giving Mrs Paton a fright.

'Sorry – I'd better go now. I really need to go round to the police station and see what's happening there.'

'I would come with you, only I'm waiting in for the window-cleaner,' said Mrs Paton, making a good recovery.

'I expect this is just some mistake,' said Pamela.

The older woman's pale blue eyes met hers, with an expression of scepticism mingled with sympathy.

'I hope you're right about that,' she said. 'Tell him I was asking for him, if you get to see him.'

'I'll do that,' said Pamela. 'Thank you.'

She wasn't at all confident about finding her way to the police station despite their previous visit there, but she muddled along and, only a few minutes after leaving Mrs Paton's, she drew up outside, only to find the place closed up. Apparently it only opened to the public in the afternoons. She wasn't going to sit outside waiting for that. Maybe if she had really been Andy's stepmother or auntie she would have done just that, she reflected as she drove off. As it was, she felt she should at least try to think rationally about the problem. Even if the officers who had taken him away had been a bit more assertive than they should, there was no reason to believe they planned to question him as a suspect. It could be that they were just following up – at last – on what she and Andy had told them the other day.

Unfortunately she had a feeling this was something quite different and that instead of meekly driving away she should have lost her temper and battered the police station doors in with her bare hands.

She was still arguing with herself when she got home, only too well aware that she remembered almost nothing about driving there, though at least she seemed to have done it without incident. The dogs sprang out of the car as soon as she opened the driver's door, and she had to run to round them up before they sprinted into the distance. Having to chase them through Cramond would have been the last straw. She'd have been fairly confident about catching Lily, but Tiger could have been at the other end of the promenade before she even saw the river front, whichever direction he'd dashed off in.

Of course they hadn't had the walk they'd probably been expecting when she put them in the car in the first place, but she hardened her heart and gave them something to eat instead, before remembering she hadn't had lunch yet, although Mrs Paton's shortbread had been quite substantial. In a futile attempt to take her mind off Andy's plight, she went and sat at her desk for a while. Her eyes kept straying to the sofa-bed. Andy had helpfully folded up all the bedding. He really was well-trained for a teenager. And pleasant to have around, too.

It could all be too good to be true, of course. She knew that.

What might they ask him? Would Paul's double life come to light? Andy probably wouldn't say anything if asked a direct question, but what if they tricked him into mentioning what they'd worked out?

She told herself it would be for the best if the police found out. Though it might mean they decided to turn their attention to her. She could imagine their scepticism when she told them she hadn't even had the smallest suspicion about Paul's other life.

'But you must have thought something was up, Mrs Prendergast, when he started staying there during the week.'

'Did you really think it was a normal marriage, what with you hardly seeing him and living your own life with your own career?'

She even imagined a court scene in which she was on trial for Paul's murder.

'So you expect the court to believe you regarded your husband's double life with equanimity, Mrs Prendergast? And you didn't lure him down to the causeway that night with the intention of leaving him stranded there?'

She opened her eyes, which she had closed so that she could conjure up the court scene more effectively in her mind. The questions she had invented for the prosecution lawyer were ridiculous. Even if she'd really lured Paul down to the causeway, she wasn't nearly strong enough to force him on to it, and in any of various scenarios she could think of, she would have put herself at risk just as much as him. And in any case, she hadn't regarded Paul's double life with equanimity because she hadn't known anything about it.

How likely was it that she might have to try and prove that she hadn't known? Could anybody prove they hadn't known something?

Chapter 15 Mal Mitchell

Pamela didn't sleep well, not surprisingly, but after tossing and turning for half the night she fell into the kind of sleep for a few hours that left her feeling fuzzy-headed and grumpy instead of refreshed. She was in no mood to deal with visitors, so when the door-bell rang while she was in the middle of her third cup of coffee, she was very tempted to ignore it.

When she saw Detective Chief Inspector Mitchell standing on the door-step, she wished she had given in to temptation.

'May I come in for a minute or two?' he said without preamble. 'I need to check out a few points with you.'

She had no doubt that somehow he now knew about her connection with Andy and had decided to follow up on it himself instead of sending more junior officers to ask the questions. Though shouldn't he have had somebody else with him? She didn't think police officers were allowed out on their own these days. Not that he had very far to come.

'All right,' she said, 'as long as you don't tell Iris and Derek. They were angling for an invitation the last time I saw them.... Coffee?'

'I could do with one,' he admitted, following her into the kitchen.

Tiger and Lily burst in through the open back door as he entered the room, and made a huge fuss of him, cavorting round his feet and trying to jump up at him, an effort that was doomed to failure.

'Maybe I'd better shut them in the other room,' said Pamela.

'No, you're OK,' he said. 'I've met fiercer brutes.'

'I'm sure you have, in your line of work.'

She closed the back door to keep the dogs in and they sat at the kitchen table with their coffee. She didn't have any biscuits left to offer him.

'It's about the boy,' he said. 'Andy Hutchison.'

'Yes, I thought it might be.'

'This isn't an official call, by the way - well, not quite. He claims to have spent the night here, and I wanted to make sure he wasn't trying to get you into trouble for some reason.'

'To get me into trouble?'

'As I've already mentioned, we don't appreciate people getting under our feet. I just can't see why you would put the boy up under your roof if the only connection between you is that you took in his dogs for him. I haven't a clue why you would even do that, unless there was more to it than you were saying.'

'He hasn't told the police anything about our connection, then?'

This was no time to dither. Pamela knew she would have to make up her mind whether to tell him the whole story or not. She tried to work out whether revealing the real identity of Andy's father would make things better or worse for the boy.

The chief inspector shook his head. 'He's not been saying very much at all. But we need some answers from him, or he's likely to find himself in far worse trouble than he is just now.'

'Answers about what?'

'You must realise I can't tell you that.'

He fell silent, staring out of the kitchen window for a few moments. Was he hoping she would rush to fill the gap in the conversation with incriminating words? She could well imagine him using that tactic. Well, two could play at that game. She sipped her coffee and gazed down at Lily, who had settled on her feet again. Tiger sat quietly under the chief inspector's chair.

'I just don't know,' she said slowly. 'What sort of trouble is Andy in?'

'We're not sure yet. But whatever it is, you won't make it any better by concealing relevant facts from us.'

His voice was quiet and calm, but she knew he would be an implacable opponent if she chose to make him one. In the end, though, it wasn't fear or guilt that led her to give in, but a strong desire to cut through the tangle of secrets and move on with her life.

'Andy's father was my husband, Paul Prendergast,' she said. 'He went by another name – Paul Hutchison – and I didn't know anything about it until the day before yesterday.'

He sat back suddenly in his chair, spilling a few drops of coffee down the front of his jacket. So she had shocked him. She felt an obscure pleasure in having done it. So DCI Mitchell didn't know everything after all.

'Well, that's a turn-up for the books,' he said at last.

'Exactly,' said Pamela.

'How did you find out?'

Pamela told him about her sketch of Andy and the wedding photo, and then about the Glasgow studio and, reluctantly, something of the way her marriage had worked. He was less surprised by that than she had expected.

'Some marriages are better for a bit of separation,' he said sagely at that point. 'I don't think it's as uncommon as you might imagine. Look at MPs, spending half their time in London hundreds of miles away from their families. Then there are all the businessmen who commute between London and elsewhere every week.'

'There must be more who travel between Edinburgh and Glasgow every day,' she pointed out.

'I suppose so… So your late husband was a jewellery designer, was he?'

'Yes. It was what he'd always wanted to do… We met at art college.'

'And you're a bit of an artist too? The sketch of young Andy?'

'I mostly work on children's books,' she muttered.

'Good, good.'

'So that's the real connection between me and the Hutchisons,' said Pamela. 'Not just the dogs… It's a bit sordid, isn't it?'

'To be honest, I've come across much worse,' he told her. 'Prendergast did well to keep it a secret all that time, though. He could easily have slipped up.'

'He gave Joanne Hutchison my name and address,' said Pamela. 'That was how Andy knew where to bring the dogs. He found it in her address book. Paul had written it there, for emergencies.'

'That's interesting. He must have foreseen she'd need your help for some reason.'

'I don't know what kind of help he could possibly have had in mind,' said Pamela.

'Just somewhere to go – somebody to listen, maybe,' said the chief inspector. 'It sounds a bit as if he'd been expecting trouble, though.'

'They said there might be a fatal accident inquiry into his death,' said Pamela.

'I can't comment on that. It's up to the procurator fiscal now. However, you'd better give us an official statement about all this. I'll send somebody round.'

'I suppose you can't comment any more on Mrs Hutchison's death either.'

'You're right, I can't.'

It didn't seem entirely fair, when she had told him so much more than she'd intended to. But then, that was probably what the police counted on. She hoped Andy would understand why she had revealed his father's secret. If it helped to divert their interest into other channels, and get him out of the clutches of the police, then it must be justified.

'You've got to let Andy go. He's got exams in a few days' time. I can drive him to college for them.'

'We'll see,' he said.

It was annoying and yet understandable that he preferred to be cryptic about it.

'So I don't need to storm the police station and break him out of a cell,' she said.

'I strongly advise you to do no such thing.'

He left just after that stern piece of advice. She had to admit to herself that it made sense. What would the dogs do, after all, if she were to be locked up as well as Andy? They might be carted off somewhere – a police cell? The cat and dog home? – and she might never be able to get them back.

After Lily had stolen one of her lunchtime sandwiches and Tiger had chewed up her favourite gloves, she started to reconsider her priorities, or at least that was what she told them. She wasn't sure they understood, though. It was hard to tell with Yorkshire terriers.

Chapter 16 An Unexpected Return

The only thing to do next was to take the two dogs for a long walk. They needed some real exercise, otherwise they'd probably destroy the whole contents of the house by tea-time. It hadn't rained for a couple of days, so she took them to the nearest patch of woodland and risked letting them run around off the lead until her nerves wore out and she rounded them up again. There were probably all sorts of hazards they might encounter up there – rabbit holes, foxes, other dogs… Best not to think about it too much. There were so many things now that Pamela didn't want to think about that she began to worry that her mind was too full up with them for her to accommodate anything useful, such as work on her current commission.

She made herself re-focus on work as she drove them all home again. Her focus was short-lived, however. She managed about half an hour in the studio, with the dogs settled on the sofa-bed, before developing a sudden urge for something sweet to eat, and when she went through to the kitchen to raid the cupboards something happened that drove the prospect of getting any work done that day completely from her mind.

A dark shadow loomed up outside the back door. She gave a squeak of alarm and dropped the packet of biscuits she'd found in the corner of a cupboard. The contents emptied themselves all over the floor, of course. It was that kind of day.

Biscuits, however, were the least of her worries. There was a tapping sound from somewhere.

Glancing back at the dark shadow, she realised it was in the shape of a person, which was good news in the sense that it probably wasn't a ghost or other figment of her imagination, and that the person must be tapping on the door.

Why hadn't they come to the front door and rung the bell? Surely that was where any legitimate caller would start? What if this was the figure Iris and Derek had spotted in her garden the other day?

A voice, somewhat muffled by the wood and glass of the door itself, called to her,

'Mrs Prendergast? Are you there?'

She remembered belatedly that the kitchen had a window and that she might be able to see the intruder from it. By the time she got there, Andy was already peering in from outside.

Her heart seemed to leap and then return to its usual rhythm as she hurried to the door, unlocked it and opened it to admit him.

'You haven't escaped from the police station, have you?'

He laughed a little shakily. 'I thought you'd never come back – I was freezing out there… No, they let me out.'

'What did they want with you in the first place? No, sit down and I'll get you a hot chocolate first. How long have you been out in the garden?'

'I suppose it must be an hour or so. I had to pretend you were in when we got here, otherwise they might not have let me go. I told them you'd be in the garden and I'd just go round by the side gate.'

'So are you saying they released you into my custody – without even seeing for themselves whether I was at home first?'

'I don't think it's custody exactly.'

He took off his backpack and put it down in the corner, then helped Pamela to pick up the biscuits.

'Just as well the dogs weren't in here to hoover those up.'

'They're worn out. I took them up to the woods for a run and then they settled down in the studio. I was hoping to get some work done when we got back.'

Andy took a seat at the table, while Pamela put the kettle on again, for what seemed like the umpteenth time that day.

'Sorry, I didn't mean to interrupt.'

'I couldn't really concentrate anyway,' she told him, standing at the counter and watching the kettle.

'They took me round by Mrs Paton's and I got some of my things. I guess Mr Mitchell spoke to them about living here. She's going to keep my room for me, though.'

'I had a nice chat with her.'

There was a long pause, which reminded her of the conversation with the chief inspector. She got out the jar of hot chocolate powder and spooned some into a mug for him.

Then Andy spoke.

'They'd been checking Mum's phone records – to try and find out who she was speaking to when – when the accident happened… So at least we stirred something up, going to see them that time.'

'Did they find out anything interesting?' asked Pamela.

'Yes, I suppose so.'

She finished pouring in the water, and gave the drink a vigorous stir. She put it on the table in front of him. He glanced up at her.

'It was me,' he said.

'What was you?'

'I was the one she was on the phone to that day... Only it wasn't me.'

'What?'

'I'd lost my phone the week before and she'd got me a new cheaper one. I've still got that. Here.' He waved a phone in front of her. It looked much the same as any other mobile phone to her, but then she wasn't a teenager.

'So – somebody else called her from your phone?'

'Yes. It took me a while to get them to understand.'

'I'm sure it did.'

'Of course they don't know who it was – assuming it wasn't me – but it's interesting, isn't it? Maybe somebody stole it on purpose so they could do that.'

'Is that what the police think?'

He shrugged. 'I don't know what they think. But they let me go, so at least I'm in the clear.'

'But if they stole it so that they could call your Mum pretending to be you, did they deliberately make the call while she was crossing the road? And how did they know she was going to cross the road at all? Everybody seems to think she always caught the bus from the same side, the side where you lived.'

'I don't know. But it's something, isn't it?'

'I suppose it means they're looking at the case a bit more carefully,' Pamela conceded.

She sat down again opposite him.

'When did you last have the phone? Can you remember?' she asked.

'They asked me that too,' he said. 'I thought I had it on the bus to college one Tuesday morning. It was maths day and I was looking at the textbook on the way. I nearly missed the stop and I had to push past some people who were getting on before he closed the doors again. I thought it might have fallen out of my pocket then.'

'Was there anybody you knew on the same bus?'

'Don't think so. But then I've not got to know that many people around here. I knew some from college, but they weren't on that bus, for definite.'

'Did you notice the phone was missing some time that day?'

'That's another thing. Usually I would've called Mum to say I was on my way home later but she told me not to bother that day because she'd be out.'

'So you usually called her?'

Andy sat back in the chair and stared at her.

'You should be in the police, Mrs Prendergast, with all those questions.'

'Sorry,' said Pamela. 'I just wanted to get it all straight in my head.' She sipped at her hot chocolate before continuing. 'Where was it you caught the bus to college?'

'It was the stop near where we lived. I used to go one way in the mornings and Mum went the other way.'

'I suppose somebody could have followed you on to the bus from there without you noticing,' she mused, half to herself. 'Or maybe they just took advantage of the situation and picked up your phone when you dropped it. Then after that they worked out how they could use it.'

He shivered.

'Drink up your hot chocolate,' she advised.

She doubted if hot chocolate alone was enough to fight off the chill that had seized him. Maybe it was a mistake to pursue this. Maybe she should encourage him to forget instead. Let sleeping dogs lie. Only those dogs weren't actually sleeping, of course, even if Tiger and Lily currently were.

Chapter 17 Rearranging the Furniture

With a sense of rearranging the deckchairs on the Titanic, Pamela decided to spend the rest of the day clearing enough space in her box-room to move the sofa-bed in there and turn it into Andy's room, at least for the duration. There was no way she would be able to call the studio her own otherwise, and she was reluctant to let him go back to Mrs Paton's until at least some of the outstanding questions could be answered. She dragged a few of the boxes into the studio and piled up the rest in a corner. Who knew when she'd have time to unpack any more of them?

Andy requested that she should paint him a happy bunny mural to make him feel at home, an idea she treated with the derision he obviously expected, and once the bed was in there she noticed he had made himself a sign for the door – 'Andy's Room' in ornate lettering with manga-style figures prancing round the edges.

He seemed to be trying to take her mind off things, just as she had decided to try and do the same for him.

Tiger and Lily had moved into the box-room along with the sofa-bed, and showed no sign of wanting to return to the studio. Still, she thought, they'd soon work out who fed and exercised them, so she had no need to be jealous.

It would have been nice not to be interrupted again after that. Andy seemed to like having his own space, and Pamela certainly appreciated being able to work at her desk without constant reminders that her house was no longer her own. She became so immersed in her work that, although she heard the front door-bell ring, it took a few minutes for her to register what the sound meant.

Not the police, please, she thought as she got up and trudged to the door, feeling with each step as if she had to drag her foot out of a swamp or a huge bowl of treacle.

Of course it wasn't the police who waited on the step, but Iris from next-door.

'Oh, Mrs Prendergast!' gasped the woman. 'I just wanted to tell you right away – Derek saw the intruder again just now. The one who climbed over the wall the other day – remember I mentioned it? He did it again. I've been on at Derek to get somebody to move that rock at the far side. Anyway, he did exactly what he did last time – ran right across our garden, and over your fence like an Olympic athlete. Only wearing a dark tracksuit with the hood up, of course. I thought I'd come and let you know in case you could catch him in the act. If you run through and open the back door now you might take him by surprise – only I'd need to come with you, of course. I wouldn't want you doing it on your own.'

By the time Iris had finished speaking, Pamela thought any intruder would be long gone anyway. She couldn't have the woman invading her house, though, so she said firmly,

'It's fine. I'll scream if I find him there, don't worry. But thanks for letting me know.'

She closed the door almost in Iris's face and went to see if Andy would join her in an expedition to the back garden. There was nobody there, of course, but the dogs were happy to be allowed out for a scamper around, and Andy was interested enough to go and look over the wall at the end of the garden and even to propose putting broken glass on top, a suggestion vetoed immediately by Pamela.

Had Iris and Derek really seen anybody there? It was odd that they would make up something like that. On the other hand, there was no sign of anybody having been in the garden – no helpfully trampled tulips, or footprints in the borders. Whoever it was could just have trodden very carefully, of course.

She didn't think the chief inspector would have been at all happy about the broken glass idea, although of course it was nothing to do with him in the first place. Or was it? She wondered if her revelations of that morning might open the door to further questions from the police. He'd said he would send somebody round to take a statement, but he'd given no indication of how urgent it was for the police to obtain this. After the day she'd just had, she thought finding the police on her doorstep might just be the last straw. Although maybe no worse than seeing Iris there.

The dogs were keen to get back into the house for their next meal, and by the look of him so was Andy. She would have to steel herself and go to a supermarket in the near future, to keep up with all their appetites. After living mostly on her own for years, Pamela realised that having others in the house, even if some of them were dogs, was bound to mean extra work one way or another, though she was surprised to find herself enjoying the company, for the moment at least.

Andy went off to college the following day, and Pamela found herself beginning to get restless in mid-morning. It had been raining all day, so she was reluctant to take the dogs to the woods, but when the skies began to clear a little she decided to drive down to Silverknowes and risk breaking cover by taking them for an airing on the promenade.

It would surely be too much of a coincidence if she bumped into Caitlin again, or saw the men who had chased Andy, or the one who had tried to abduct Tiger. That was what she told herself, anyway.

She parked the car and walked down the slope past the café without incident. So far, so good. Maybe she should just park herself too, at one of the outside tables, and sit there for a while. If anything went wrong she could call on the friendly waiter or even another customer.

'I can't let them control me,' she muttered to herself, walking resolutely past the tables and on to the promenade. Tiger and Lily between them were trying to pull her in two different directions. So much for not letting anybody else control her. Did she have to resign herself now to being at the mercy of these small terriers?

'... mustn't let them control you,' said a woman's voice somewhere nearby.

Pamela glanced round. A woman was staring at her from only a few feet away, her expression critical.

'You're the leader of the pack – the one who pulls the strings, or in this case the leads,' she said. 'Make that clear to them. They're to stop when you decide to stop. If you want a coffee, they're going to have to wait patiently while you have one. If they want to carry on walking but you've had enough, they just have to turn round and go with you. And without getting their leads tangled up, either.'

The woman's own dog, apparently a different kind of terrier, sat patiently at her side, a somewhat martyred expression on its hairy, greying face.

'Just because Yorkies have been bred to look cute and winning, doesn't mean they're exempt from the rules of being a dog,' the woman continued, 'and neither are you exempt from your duties as g a dog owner.'

'Of course not,' Pamela stammered.

Somehow this woman seemed to have been conjured up out of thin air to provide unsolicited dog advice. Pamela supposed if anybody needed it she did. On the other hand, she had never taken kindly to unsolicited advice about anything. Sometimes it might have been better if she had.

Did the woman lurk about here on purpose to catch beginners with their dogs? Maybe she was even there to advertise dog training classes. Any minute now, she would hand Pamela a leaflet and advise her to come along to the nearest church hall on Thursday evenings to spend an hour with various misbehaving dogs and their owners. It sounded like one of the worst circles of hell.

'I'd better get on,' she said.

The woman laughed, and all at once the angular face had softened and she looked a lot more human and a lot less like a Victorian school mistress.

'Sorry,' she chortled. 'I didn't mean to come out with all that at once. I just get so frustrated seeing people who could do better for their dogs and themselves.'

'That's all right,' said Pamela, although it wasn't. 'You're right, I'm a complete beginner. I didn't even choose to acquire the dogs in the first place.'

The other woman sobered up quickly. 'You didn't inherit them or something, did you? That's always difficult.'

'Well, sort of. But it's a bit too complicated to explain just now.'

'I'm just heading along that way – towards Cramond, I mean. Wrong time to get out to the island, of course, but I thought I'd go up river a bit with Kenny and then circle back. We could walk along together, if you'd like to talk about the dogs a bit more.'

She bent down and reached out a hand to Tiger, who fortunately didn't live up to his name but sniffed at her and wagged his tail. Lily cowered behind Pamela's legs.

'I don't think,' Pamela began. 'I was planning to walk the other way, but...'

Great. Now she had shown herself to be just as indecisive and woolly as the woman had first thought. She wasn't even in control of her own actions, never mind those of the dogs.

'That's all right,' said the woman. 'But if you have any trouble with them, do think about giving me a call. I'm a dog psychologist by trade. Well, a vet really, but I specialise in problem dogs – and their owners.'

She chuckled again. Pamela couldn't make up her mind whether the sound was reassuring or sinister.

'I shouldn't really give people advice without booking them in for a session. My daughter's always telling me off for sticking my nose into things. Too much time with dogs, I suppose. Here – take my card in case you ever need it.'

Pamela took the business card and stuffed it in her pocket.

'Thanks, Mrs – um. I'm Pamela Prendergast.'

She'd forgotten even to look at the name on the card, but the woman filled the awkward pause neatly.

'Eleanor Sharp. I mostly see patients at the practice but I can come to you if that would be more convenient.'

'Thanks. Well, I'd better get on now. It isn't that I don't need advice,' she added just before turning away. 'But I'd have to think about it first.'

'I understand,' said Eleanor Sharp.

Perhaps the chuckle had been reassuring after all. Still, as Pamela walked away with Tiger and Lily, heading as usual away from the view of Cramond Island, she was conscious that Eleanor was still watching her and possibly even mentally critiquing the pace she walked at, or the shoes she was wearing, or the fact that Lily tended to lag behind a little while Tiger ran ahead, or almost anything about her.

Pamela didn't relax until she had walked on round the curve of the promenade and could be reasonably sure of being out of sight. Even then she could only relax for a moment or two, because at this point she realised there was nobody else about and that she would have nobody to turn to for help if she or the dogs were to be accosted by any of the people who had chased Andy or attempted to abduct Tiger, or by Caitlin and her partner – or the mysterious intruder in the garden, of whose existence she was not entirely convinced.

On the other hand, there was no sign of any of these people either. She told herself she couldn't live the rest of her life wondering if somebody was going to spring out at her out of nowhere. She didn't even have any evidence that any of them had intended serious harm. Still, maybe she should keep away from the promenade until some of the mysteries around Joanne Hutchison's death had been cleared up.

On this thought she decided to turn back.

It was the wrong decision. Caitlin waited for her at the foot of the slope that led up to the road and the safety of Pamela's car.

Caitlin didn't waste any words. She handed something to Pamela.

'This is for Andy Hutchison – if you happen to see him.'

There was a kind of sneer in the words, as if Caitlin knew exactly where Andy was staying now, and both resented it and took pleasure in the knowledge of his whereabouts.

Pamela took the thing – it was wrapped in a plastic bag – and went on up the slope without speaking. Luckily the dogs didn't seem inclined to make any fuss of Caitlin either.

She had no qualms about unwrapping the thing Caitlin had given her, once she was in the car. It was a mobile phone. She guessed it was Andy's old phone, the one he'd lost. The one that might have been used to lure his mother to her death.

Pamela supposed she'd have to give it to him, although it should probably be handed straight over to the police. There might be information on it that they couldn't retrieve from phone records. She didn't fully understand how these things worked.

The police! She suddenly recalled what DCI Mitchell had said about the official statement. They could even now be on her doorstep, ringing her door-bell and wondering where she'd got to, or driving back to the station in a huff because she'd wasted their time.

Though accidentally missing their visit would be a better option than having to make the statement while having the lost phone concealed somewhere in the house like a tell-tale heart. She doubted whether she'd be able to stop herself from telling them about it.

She would have to tell them, even if it wasn't exactly relevant to their reason for speaking to her.

As it turned out, there was a police car sitting outside the bungalow when she turned into her street. She had a silly urge to execute a fast u-turn and drive off to somewhere else – almost anywhere would do. Only the thought of triggering a car chase stopped her from doing it. She had never had any wish to take part in one.

She could just imagine Iris and Derek enjoying the view from their front window, too. How long would it be before one of them rang the door-bell and tried to find out what was going on?

She parked in the drive and got herself and the dogs out. Two uniformed police officers, a man and a woman, emerged from their car.

'Mrs Prendergast?' said the woman. She introduced them – she was the more senior, apparently. 'DCI Mitchell asked us to take a statement from you.'

'Yes,' said Pamela. 'You'd better come in. Sorry to have kept you waiting.'

'It hasn't been very long,' said the male officer politely.

She showed them into the front room and shut the dogs in the kitchen with fresh water and some dog biscuits. Even Eleanor Sharp couldn't accuse her of neglecting their needs, surely.

The detective inspector must have told them what to ask her. It was easier than she had expected to get through the statement – maybe if she told enough people about Paul's double life, the tale would eventually become boring enough for her to regard it as something slightly unusual that had happened to somebody else and not to her at all.

At the end of the interview she said,

'There's something else here that I think you might be interested in.'

She took the phone, which she had re-wrapped, out of her pocket and put it on the coffee table between them, mentally apologising to Andy who might reasonably have wanted to have it back.

'Where did you get this?' enquired the woman officer, without touching it.

'I'm guessing it must be Andy Hutchison's phone – somebody gave me it. At the beach at Silverknowes.'

'Mmhm,' said the male officer. 'Anybody you know?'

'I wouldn't say I know her, exactly,' said Pamela, somehow reluctant to get Caitlin into any trouble, although she supposed she shouldn't really have any scruples about doing that.

'Have you got a name?' asked the woman officer.

'She said she was Caitlin French. I've bumped into her a couple of times, walking the dogs along the prom at Silverknowes. I think she lives somewhere not far from there.'

'We'll have a word with her,' said the woman officer. 'Why would she give you this, though?'

'I don't know. I had a feeling she was trying to make a point.'

'What point?' asked the male officer.

He might well ask. Pamela had already debated with herself over just that question.

'She asked me to pass it on to Andy. So I suppose the point was that she knew he was staying with me.'

The woman officer frowned. 'Did you feel threatened?'

'Not particularly,' Pamela lied.

'Really?'

'Well, maybe just a bit.'

'We'll definitely have a word,' said the woman officer. 'I wouldn't go there again for now, though. We know she has friends.'

'Friends?'

This almost came out as a squeak, but Pamela managed to tone it down a little at the last minute.

'They're not very nice,' said the male officer.

'Don't worry, though,' said the woman. 'You'll be all right here, what with the chief living next-door and everything… Just be careful where you take the dogs, all right? Until we get this all sorted.'

'Thanks,' said Pamela, although she didn't really feel thankful. The last thing she needed was another reason to feel anxious every time she closed the front door behind her on the way out.

'You should put your car away in the garage too,' the male officer advised. 'You wouldn't' want to get up one morning and find the tyres slashed or the windows broken.'

'All right, thanks.'

He picked up the plastic bag with the phone in and they left, checking the lock on the front door on their way out to see if they approved of it.

Pamela was quite glad to have them and Andy's phone off the premises, but she worried over the fact that they would now go and question Caitlin again, giving the woman another reason to resent her.

It was well past any reasonable lunchtime by then, so she grabbed a lump of cheese and a couple of small tomatoes and ate them quickly in the kitchen, washed down with a can of cola she'd bought for Andy. There were a couple of biscuits left, so she finished the snack – it hardly even deserved that title – with those, and then realised she'd have to go and stock up on dog food and something more substantial for Andy before the end of the day. She would have preferred to wait so that he could come with her and choose what he wanted to eat, but he hadn't got back from college and the day was getting on, so she went off alone, feeling as nervous as if she were exploring the Antarctic and not just driving to a run-of-the-mill supermarket a few streets away.

Maybe it would have been better to send Andy back to Mrs Paton's, and trust that he would be all right there. Maybe he would be safer at Mrs Paton's. As she parked the car, Pamela asked herself if the boy's safety was really what she was worried about.

The following day she had reason to doubt her own motives all over again.

Chapter 18 Invasion

Andy was still asleep when Pamela took the dogs out in the morning. She had happened to catch the weather forecast on the radio and knew she had to go early to avoid the rain. As it was, when she came out of the woods a couple of drops landed on her face, and by the time she arrived home the windscreen wipers were working hard.

She couldn't remember being so conscious of the weather when she'd lived in the New Town. Of course she hadn't had the dogs then. Living there, they'd have had to settle for short mundane walks in the city parks and gardens where they were allowed. No wild scampering in the woods or unsettling encounters on the shore.

She was pleased to see Andy in the kitchen. He'd even got himself some breakfast. The dogs immediately stationed themselves under the table at his feet, probably hoping for cereal crumbs.

'I raided the cupboards,' he said. 'Sorry – hope that was all right.'

'It's good – I'm glad you found something,' she said, wandering over to see if the kettle was hot. She could do with a coffee.

'Your neighbour came in,' he said. 'Not the chief inspector – a woman.'

'Came in?'

There had been an odd hint of disapproval in his tone.

He nodded. 'She let herself in. With a key,' he added, to underline the point.

'With a key? I didn't know anybody had a key!'

Pamela really needed her coffee in the mornings, so she got herself a cup before settling down at the table to find out more.

'Was it Iris?'

'She didn't say. But she wrote you a note. It's on that shelf by the front door.'

'Did you speak to her at all?'

'Just to ask what she was doing in here, and she said she had always had a key and she thought you'd be glad of having a neighbour who had one for emergencies, being on your own… I didn't think you'd be glad, but I didn't say that to her.'

'Good – I'd better ask her for it. She shouldn't have kept it in the first place.'

'Or you could get the locks changed,' said Andy calmly. He spooned up the last of the cereal and sat back in the chair. The dogs, looking disappointed, came out from under the table and went to see if there was anything in either of their food dishes. Tiger had a very noisy drink of water, maybe to make a point of some kind.

'I don't want to go to that much bother.'

'What if they give you the key back but they've had another copy made?'

'Mmm. Why would they do that?'

He shrugged. 'Why would they keep the key and not give it to you when you moved in? They could have asked you then if you wanted them to hang on to it.'

Andy had obviously thought this through more extensively than Pamela. But then he had had a bit more time to do so.

'I suppose I'd better read her note,' she said.

There was indeed a folded piece of paper, addressed to her in extremely neat, precise handwriting, on the shelf in the hall. Pamela took it back into the kitchen with her. Maybe she would find it easier to read – and if necessary contain her anger about the contents – in front of Andy than if she were alone.

A couple of minutes later, she put the note down on the table in front of her, glanced up at him and said,

'She's invited me round for tea.'

'Did she mean afternoon tea or a proper meal?' he asked.

'Well, she says I should come at about three o'clock this afternoon, if convenient, so I'm assuming afternoon tea.'

'Nice,' he said. 'French fancies and cucumber sandwiches cut into triangles.'

She smiled at last. 'I don't like cucumber… What do you know about afternoon tea, anyway?'

'They went out for a special tea once – Mum and Dad. They said it was for their anniversary… It couldn't have been their wedding anniversary. There probably wasn't a wedding anyway. Mum took photos of the cake stand.'

Pamela didn't know what to say about the wedding. If Paul had really married Joanne under his other name, it would have been illegal, since he was still married to her. She doubted if he would have gone as far as to commit bigamy. If he'd been found out it would have caused a huge fuss and his cover would have been well and truly blown.

Paul had never taken her out for afternoon tea. Their wedding anniversaries had been marked mostly by the ceremonial exchange of flowers and whisky. That last time she had bought her own flowers. She should have known then…

There was no way she could have known. Not the whole story, that was for sure.

'I suppose I'll have to go,' she said. 'There's going to be some very awkward conversation over the tea-cups, though, if I ask for the key.'

'You'd better do it anyway,' said Andy. 'She'll only use it again the next time we're both out, if you don't.'

'She didn't say anything about you, did she? Was she surprised to see you here?'

'She looked as if she was going to say something, but then she decided to write the note instead.'

'Oh well, that's something,' said Pamela. She wasn't looking forward to afternoon tea at all, no matter how many tiny sandwiches and dainty cakes they offered her, but at least she had right on her side in the matter of the key.

Now that she thought about it, the bungalow had been sold with vacant possession, which was one reason she and Paul had put in their offer. Maybe the previous owner had been an older person who had died or gone into a care home. That might have given Iris an excuse to keep a copy of the key, but the woman had no excuse for holding on to it once the place was sold.

She managed to get some work done despite the sense of having to psych herself up for the encounter with Iris and Derek. She wouldn't have chosen to socialise with them even if it hadn't been for the key problem. But then, wasn't there a saying about keeping your friends close and your enemies closer? Not that Iris and Derek were enemies, or at least she hoped they weren't. She just didn't see them as friends either.

Later, Iris welcomed her into the house next-door with a smile.

'I'm so glad you could fit us in today,' she said. 'You seem to be such a busy person, what with the two wee dogs, and now you've got a lodger too…'

She showed Pamela into the front room, where Derek sat in a recliner chair with a good view of the front garden and the street outside through the picture window.

'I apologise for not getting up,' he said. 'My knees…'

'His knees haven't been the same since we went on that tour of the Amalfi Coast for our holidays,' Iris added. 'Who knew there were so many steep hills there?'

Pamela would have thought looking at the map would have told them something, but she didn't want to get distracted from her main purpose here by entering into a side argument.

'Have you ever been to Italy?' Iris went on. 'We had to draw the line at Pompei and Herculaneum. But when you've seen one set of Roman ruins, you've seen them all, haven't you? I really prefer a beach holiday myself. Of course it's a while since we were able to go away anywhere much. We're looking at cruises for next year.'

She stopped talking for long enough to show Pamela to a chair. The nearby coffee table was laden with tea-cups and matching teapot, and two cake-stands, one holding the statutory triangular sandwiches and the other over-loaded with fancy cakes, scones and bite-sized pieces of fruit cake.

Pamela was glad she had arrived promptly, as Iris evidently expected her to start on the refreshments right away.

'How do you like your tea? It's only just made, so we should maybe leave it a few minutes. Or I could pour yours now if you like it weak.' Iris made it sound as if taking tea weak might be considered a serious crime. 'Derek likes his very strong, of course, typical man. And what would you like to eat? There's cream cheese and smoked salmon and ham and tomato, or maybe you're vegetarian? We've got cheddar and pickle too, if you like.'

'What a lovely selection!' said Pamela politely. She didn't drink tea at all, but she didn't want to offend Iris more than she had to by saying so.

'We had it all delivered from the cake shop,' said Iris. 'What's the place called again, Derek?'

'I don't know,' said Derek. 'Daisy's something or other? Or is it Maisie's?'

'Maisie's!' said Iris triumphantly. 'That's the one. She calls it the Calico Cat nowadays, but it was just a wee cake shop before, without all the cat bric-a-brac. She's quite a good baker. We used to go along there for afternoon tea sometimes, but we got out of the way of doing it. Much cosier to stay at home, anyway.'

Pamela didn't find their front room at all cosy. 'Suffocating' might have been a better word for it. There were lacy net curtains, and then more curtains with a busy floral pattern and flounces and ornate tie-backs. The carpet clashed with the wallpaper and the chairs were upholstered in a faded pink velvet that clashed with everything else. She told herself she couldn't afford to be so critical when most of her curtains were still in boxes and she thought she might have once had a teapot and a cake-stand somewhere but they might have been lost in the move – with any luck.

'I'll give you a bit of everything, will I?' said Iris. 'Do you like the milk in first?'

'Yes, thanks, that's fine. Not too much, though. I'm not used to eating at this time of day.'

'We'll see about that, dear,' said Iris. 'Won't we, Derek?'

Derek gave a non-committal grunt and said a moment later, 'There's Mal Mitchell on his way out again, Iris.'

'Oh, not again! What is it this time, I wonder?'

Pamela was rather horrified to know how closely Derek was monitoring the comings and goings in this quiet street. They must have known about Andy's presence well before Iris's incursion into the house that morning. She probably even knew he was still at home and hadn't gone out with Pamela and the dogs, which made her actions even more dubious in their intent than if she'd thought the house was empty.

The sandwiches were very edible. It was just the company that made her feel queasy. She had already started wondering when she could leave.

'So, how are you getting on with Andy, then?' said Iris suddenly.

Andy? Had he told her his name, or did she already know him from somewhere?

'We knew his mother,' said Derek, tearing his attention away from the window for a moment.

'Joanne,' added Iris. 'Are you ready for a scone? Or would you rather go straight on to the cake?'

'I'd better pause for a minute first, thanks,' said Pamela. She would have preferred to stuff a few scones in her pocket and head for home without delay, but even though she wasn't well versed in afternoon tea etiquette, she realised that would be a bit rude.

Iris inclined her head in a regal manner.

'It must be strange having a teenage boy about the place,' she mused aloud. 'When you're not used to it, I mean.'

'I don't think he'll be with me for long,' said Pamela.

'Derek says the police brought him back yesterday.'

'Was it only yesterday?' said Pamela. 'It seems as if it must have been longer ago. But then, there's so much going on and I've hardly had the chance to settle in yet.'

'So is it some sort of scheme, then?' said Iris.

'Scheme?'

'A bit like fostering, is it? Looking after somebody for a while until they're ready to look after themselves?'

'It isn't quite like that,' said Pamela, hoping a firm reply would pre-empt more questions along these lines.

Interesting, she thought. Iris obviously hadn't sussed out her real connection with Andy, and she was poking around in whatever way she could to find it out. Was it because she liked to pry pointlessly into other people's affairs, or was there something else behind her interest?

'So what do you do, Pamela?' asked Iris.

'What do I do? Oh, for a living, you mean. I'm an illustrator.'

'An illustrator?'

'Mostly children's books,' said Pamela, trying to sound proud of her profession and not modest about it, which was her more natural stance.

'Not much money in that kind of thing, is there?' growled Derek.

Iris frowned at him. 'What kind of question is that, Derek? You'll embarrass Pamela.'

'That's all right,' said Pamela. 'The money depends on getting commissions, usually, but I'm hoping to branch out into writing and illustrating my own books. For children.'

'That's nice,' said Iris absently.

She was playing with her big necklace, and the pieces of it made clunking noises as they came together. The discordant notes made a fitting accompaniment to this awkward visit.

'What made you decide to move to Cramond?' Iris asked.

'My late husband and I had decided to move not long before he died. Everything was signed and sealed, and I thought it would be easier to carry on than to try and unravel it. Anyway, I'm glad of the change of scenery.'

'And more space to walk your wee dogs,' said Iris.

Pamela opened her mouth to say she hadn't had the dogs when she lived in the New Town, but she changed her mind at the last minute, following some instinct that told her not to divulge too many details to this pair.

'That's true – quite a few different options here,' she said instead.

'There's some nice walks along the river,' said Iris, 'and then if you check the tides you can get out to the island along the causeway.'

Pamela almost succeeded in suppressing a shudder, but she had a feeling Iris's sharp, bright eyes had noticed it.

'Do you go that way very often?' she asked.

'Well, we used to walk down to the boat, but Derek can't make it that far on foot now, so we take the car down.'

'Down to the boat?'

'Yes, we've kept a boat there for years. We don't get out in it as much now, though. We were thinking of selling it this coming season – in case you're interested?'

'Our Katie's not interested at all,' remarked Derek. 'Or we could've passed it on to her.'

Iris ignored this and spoke to Pamela again.

'It's a lovely location, and there are some nice outings along the coastline and round the islands. You don't even need to go very far.'

'I wouldn't know which end of a boat was which,' said Pamela. 'You must have had some interesting times in it, though,' she added politely.

'Interesting – yes. The Forth can be quite tricky, even once you think you know every last rock and current,' said Derek.

Between them they came up with a list of boating reminiscences, some more nerve-racking than others. Pamela had no opportunity to make an excuse and leave until Iris glanced at her watch and said,

'We've kept you here far too long! Isn't it nice when you don't notice the time passing? But I'm sure your lodger will be wondering where you've got to.'

This was a definite cue for her to leave, thank goodness. Pamela got up and was on the point of going when she remembered the key. This would be the most awkward part of the conversation, she knew.

'I just wanted to ask about the key,' she said, plunging in at the deep end.

'The key?' said Iris, eyes wide and innocent now.

'I didn't realise you'd been kind enough to keep a front door key with you for the previous owner of my house,' said Pamela. 'I don't think I'll need you to do that any longer.'

She waited. Iris gazed at her. The woman must surely understand what she was saying. Or was she deliberately trying to force Pamela to ask for it directly?

'I didn't know we still had the key, Iris,' said Derek, interrupting the stand-off. 'You'd better find it for Pamela.'

'Thanks,' said Pamela. 'I wouldn't want you to have the responsibility of looking after it.'

'But with you being on your own and everything…'

'Iris,' said Derek. 'Where have you put the key?'

Iris glared at her husband. 'I suppose it must be in the hall table drawer. I'll give it to Pamela on her way out.'

'Just you do that,' said Derek. He leaned forward in the recliner chair. 'There's Mal Mitchell coming back again already. He's maybe just been to the shops.'

'I don't know why we're so interested in Mal Mitchell's movements all of a sudden,' said Iris crossly.

She ushered Pamela out to the hall, opened the drawer in the table with a crash and took out the key.

'Here you are – if you're sure you don't want us to keep it for emergencies.'

'I'll just have to try not to have any emergencies.'

'Well, you never know when something might happen,' said Iris. 'Still, it's up to you.'

'Thank you for the lovely tea,' said Pamela, taking the key and tucking it in her pocket. 'It was really - outstanding.'

The whole experience had been outstanding, though not in a good way. She gave the spare key to Andy to save him from having to loom up at the back door and give her a fright the next time he was locked out, and told him enough about the tea-party to male him alternately laugh and hide his face in mock horror.

'Had you ever met Iris before she barged into the house today?' she asked at the end of her account.

He shook his head. 'Not that I know.'

'Did you tell her your name?'

'Definitely not.'

'She seemed to know it. I wonder how that happened... No, wait a minute. She claimed to have known your mother.'

'Claimed?' said Andy. 'You didn't believe her, then?'

'It seemed odd. I don't see how their paths could have crossed.'

'Maybe she's well in with the Chief Inspector too,' Andy suggested. 'Maybe she's had him to tea.'

'Had him for breakfast, more like,' said Pamela.

Andy just started to laugh again, although it hadn't been all that funny.

Chapter 19 Even More Questions

Pamela knew she had to get on with her work, otherwise she would miss a couple of deadlines, so she was particularly annoyed to hear the door-bell not long after noon on the day after the awkward tea-party. She couldn't bring herself to ignore it. If she happened to find Iris on the door-step, she would be strongly tempted to close the door in the woman's face. Apart from anything else, she had never had the desire to make friends with her neighbours. There was no reason for them to have much in common apart from living in the same street, or the same area, and she knew from her experience of the New Town that the geographical proximity caused as many problems as it solved, if not more. She guessed this was even more likely here, where there were garden fences and yapping dogs to fall out with the neighbours over. Of course she didn't want to make enemies either, she reasoned with herself on the way to the door, but there must be a happy medium somewhere.

Detective Chief Inspector Mitchell stood outside the front door, accompanied by the woman officer she'd seen the previous day.

This was a bit of an escalation, which put her on the alert from the start.

'I'm afraid we need to ask you a few more questions,' said Mitchell, his tone apologetic. 'Is Andrew Hutchison with you?'

'He's staying here, yes,' said Pamela. 'But he's out at college just now. His maths exam's in a few days.'

'Can we come in anyway?' said Mitchell. 'We need to clear up a few things with you too.'

She led them into the front room. Unfortunately she'd forgotten the dogs had settled down, in separate chairs, after their walk in the grounds of Lauriston Castle earlier in the day. They jumped down and yapped round the feet of the two police officers.

'If you just sit down they'll stop eventually,' said Pamela. 'Or would you rather I put them in another room?'

If anything she decided she might feel more at ease if the dogs stayed. That would give her something else to think about other than the Chief Inspector's grim expression.

'It's all right,' said the woman officer. 'They're not going to savage us, are you, darling?'

She had bent down to pat Tiger, and her last words were obviously meant for him. Pamela caught the Chief Inspector rolling his eyes. At least it made him appear almost human.

The two of them sat down. Lily seemed to take a liking to Mitchell, for she sat on his feet. Pamela perched on the window-seat facing them. She would have liked to stay on her feet, partly in order to give herself a bit of a start on them if she needed to take to her heels and run away - though she guessed the woman officer at least must be ten years younger than she was, and much more athletic.

'I've read your statement through, but there are a couple of things I need to get clear in my mind,' said the Chief Inspector.

'I don't know anything more about Mrs Hutchison's accident,' she said.

'It isn't about that,' he told her.

'Oh – sorry, I thought that's what you'd come about. I thought it might be to do with Andy's phone.'

'Thanks for handing it over, by the way. It confirmed what we already knew about the call that was made. Not who made it, of course. But young Andy is quite certain he lost it well before the day of the accident, and we have no reason to disbelieve him… This is about your late husband, Paul Prendergast.'

He paused. Had there been something portentous about the way he'd said Paul's name, or was she imagining things again?

'Would it surprise you to learn,' he went on, 'that he may have been involved in criminal activity?'

'Criminal…? Well, yes, of course it would.'

Even as Pamela spoke, she remembered the gems – or pieces of coloured glass – she and Andy had found in the box. There had been no time even to think any more about them, what with Andy's college work, her own work, Iris's house invasion, having to walk the dogs somewhere different every day…

'Did it have something to do with the jewellery?' she asked.

He blinked. 'Yes, it was, as it happens. Was that just a lucky guess, or what?'

'Sort of. It was the only thing I could think of that might explain some of what happened… The move to a different studio in Glasgow and then back to Edinburgh. The fact that somebody tried to abduct one of the dogs while I was out with them. And there's been somebody in the garden – at least, that's what Iris and Derek said.'

'Iris and Derek Goodfellow. Mmhm,' he said.

'As far as I knew,' she continued, 'Paul was just doing what he'd always done, ever since leaving art college. Making designer jewellery. But maybe there was more to it than that.'

'I'm afraid there's money to be made in melting down jewellery and putting the gems into new settings,' said the Chief Inspector. 'A man might be tempted to go in for that – especially if he had two households to maintain.'

Pamela blushed, feeling obscurely guilty. Maybe the best thing she could have done for Paul would have been to divorce him, which would at least have left him with only one household to keep up. On the other hand, he had never asked for that, and she hadn't even imagined there was anything odd about their relationship. There must have been something he liked about her and their home – or was it just having a base in the New Town he enjoyed? They'd always gone out and about on Saturdays, attending concerts and going to the theatre. They were within easy reach of galleries, and were often among the early visitors to various exhibitions. His life with Joanne and Andy must have been a completely different life. If only he'd settled for one life instead of two, he'd probably still have been alive to enjoy it.

She suddenly realised there had been a long silence. Was it her turn to speak? She couldn't say any of the things that had been milling around in her mind, so she tried to pick up the conversational thread in a slightly different way.

'We found some stones in a box here,' she said. 'I'd overlooked some of Paul's things when I was tidying up before moving house. There was a little drawstring bag of them. I have no idea whether they were rubies and diamonds or glass beads. Would you like to see them?'

DCI Mitchell gave a heavy sigh, as if he would really have preferred not to bother with jewellery because he had enough on his plate already – which could well be true, for all she knew.

'We'd have to hand them over to the team dealing with that side of things,' he said. 'You might not get them back for some time – if ever.'

She shook her head. 'I don't mind that. I don't want them back anyway, if there's any chance of them having been stolen.'

'Did your late husband ever give you presents of jewellery?' he asked suddenly.

Pamela recoiled, horrified. In fact Paul had never given her anything like that – flowers, theatre tickets, occasionally gadgets for the kitchen… Now that she thought about it all his gifts had an impersonal touch about them. Even if he'd wanted to give her something to wear, he would have presented her with a gift voucher for a good shop. But if he'd ever thought of giving her the proceeds of crime… It was an unwelcome idea. She supposed her reaction to it was over the top, though. Mitchell was giving her an odd look.

'No, never,' she said.

Had Paul given anything like that to Joanne Hutchison? She didn't really want the image of him lovingly arranging a glittering necklace round the woman's neck even to cross her mind. It was hard to conjure up a picture of the two of them together anyway, since she didn't know what Joanne had looked like. Andy probably had a photo of his mother somewhere but in a way she didn't want to know.

'I'll go and fetch the things we found,' she added, forcing herself to get off the window-seat and cross to the door.

'Thank you for your co-operation,' said the Chief Inspector.

She paused in the act of opening the door. It almost sounded as if he had finished the questions.

'We'll be going,' he added. 'But you must understand that because we have this information, we may now have to look at your late husband's death in a different light.'

'Yes?' she said, now desperate for them to leave her alone.

'We saw it as an accident in the first place but you should be aware that we may now have to open a murder investigation.'

Pamela clutched the door-handle in an effort to stay on her feet. Her legs were trembling and she was afraid they wouldn't carry her even as far as the hall.

'Are you all right, Mrs Prendergast?' asked the woman officer.

'I'll be fine in a minute. I just didn't think…'

She pulled herself together and opened the door. 'I'll get you the gems.'

Andy came in through the front door as they all went into the hall. He glanced from Pamela to the police officers and back.

'What's wrong?'

'I'll explain it all in a bit,' said Pamela.

Andy followed her into the box-room – his room – and watched as she picked up the little drawstring bag from the window-sill, where they had rather carelessly left it.

'What's this about?'

'It's complicated. Wait until they've gone.'

'They've upset you.'

'It's not their fault,' she told him, conscious that he had clenched his fists. It was touching in a way that he seemed to be ready to spring to her defence, but she didn't want him to get into any further trouble.

The dogs had followed the two officers to the front door, where they stood waiting to leave.

'Can you catch the dogs?' said Pamela to Andy. 'I don't want them running outside.'

Andy, silent and solemn, picked up a dog in each hand and carried them into the kitchen.

'Thank you very much, Mrs Prendergast,' said Mitchell as she handed over the little bag. 'We'll try not to bother you again unless we have to.'

'No problem,' said Pamela. She closed the front door after them, and leaned against it.

Once they started on the murder investigation, nobody would have any secrets from them. She imagined the ripples from it spreading, engulfing both her and Andy and ruining both their lives. Every last sordid detail of Paul's double life would come out in court eventually, and...

It was too much like a nightmare to contemplate. She pushed herself upright again and stalked towards the kitchen. This was definitely a situation that called for ample quantities of coffee and whole packets of biscuits, wolfed down without touching the sides.

Chapter 20 Amateur Sleuths

Andy was up for helping with the biscuits, but he didn't see that there was anything to be done about the rest of it. But then, he was young and unable at present to look beyond the exams that cast their shadow over his immediate future. Pamela hesitated to come right out and suggest that the police might need all the help they could get, so she approached the subject in a slightly different way.

'Why don't we take the dogs down to the Almond walkway this afternoon? It'd be a nice change of scenery – I haven't been that way since last week, and it's quite safe for the dogs. Apart from the river, of course.'

'All right,' said Andy. 'But didn't you want to avoid the river mouth because…'

'Well, sort of,' said Pamela. 'But I think I might be ready for it now. We can see if we feel like having a closer look at the causeway once we get there.'

Oddly enough, now that Paul's secret double life had been exposed, not to mention that the police had used the word 'murder', Pamela felt less squeamish about possibly seeing the place where he had died. Or at least, where his body had been found. Maybe it was turning into an episode in one of these television detective dramas in which they had to work out where the actual murder had taken place and how the body had been moved, and so on. She shuddered, realising she felt far more squeamish about this development in real life than she might have done while watching tv.

'Well, if you're sure,' said Andy, apparently not quite convinced. 'But maybe there's another way we can go if you change your mind.'

'I'm sure there is,' said Pamela.

They set off on foot this time. It wouldn't do any of them, including the dogs, any harm to walk a little further than usual. When they reached the river bank and saw the mud under foot, Pamela almost had second thoughts, knowing she might have to bathe the two dogs later, but maybe she could persuade them to rinse themselves off in the water somewhere, if there was a spot where it wasn't flowing so fast.

They climbed a flight of steep steps and then descended another set, and then there was a weir. So much for finding a slower-flowing place in the river, Pamela mused, as they all stood still for a while watching and listening to the torrent.

Walking on, the path led them through a woodland area and then they passed a boatyard.

'Iris said something about a boat,' she mused aloud. 'She and Derek have one somewhere here. I wonder if it's one of these.'

There were boats on the river itself too. She had trouble connecting Iris and boats in her mind, especially after seeing the interior of the house next-door. But maybe it was really Derek's hobby. Wouldn't he have trouble keeping his balance on a boat, though?

She took out her phone for a couple of photos. There were picturesque houses at the landward side of the path, and a view of the Firth of Forth opened out in front of them.

Pamela steeled herself to walk on towards the start of the causeway.

'Looks like the tide's in,' said Andy. He paused by the notice-board. 'Here's the tide times.'

'Why would anybody set out across the causeway when the tide was coming in?' said Pamela, half to herself.

'Maybe he'd been drinking,' suggested Andy.

'Paul never drank much,' said Pamela, on the defensive now.

Andy laughed. 'Are you sure he was the same man as my Dad? He was at the pub every other night.'

'Really?'

'Yes.'

'Not at weekends,' said Pamela.

He'd been on his best behaviour with her, evidently. In a way she even resented him for that. He hadn't been able to relax and be himself. No wonder he'd looked for an alternative. Still, whatever he'd thought the problems were between them, he'd chosen a silly way of resolving them.

'It wasn't your fault,' said Andy, as if reading her thoughts.

Were her facial expressions so transparent?

They walked to the end of the stone wall that led to the start of the causeway, and stared down at the water and the line of concrete posts sticking up from it at intervals all the way to the island. Somewhere along there Paul had died – or possibly somewhere else. Pamela used her phone again to take a couple of quick photos.

She couldn't even bring herself to shed a single tear. What kind of unnatural woman was she? The least she should have done was to sense his spectral presence out there, hovering above the water, or maybe rising up out of it like a playful dolphin.

Without any warning, she wanted to get that image down on paper before it left her.

'Let's go home now. We can go up past the church. It'll be a bit quicker than the way we came.'

He gave her a worried sidelong look, but didn't say anything.

'I've been wondering if there's a short cut,' she told him. 'Past the Roman fort and the church and across the bit of land behind my house. But I don't want to come to a dead end and have to re-trace my steps.'

'I don't think the dogs would be up for that either,' said Andy, looking down at them. Lily was making heavy weather of the walk up the hill from the foreshore, and even Tiger wasn't tugging to get ahead as he usually did.

'Oh dear,' said Pamela. 'I'd better carry Lily a bit of the way. I think we've walked their legs off.'

Andy scooped up Lily and after wriggling a little she settled into his grasp.

'Let Tiger walk on for a bit,' he advised.

'I don't want him holding us up. I need to get home.'

'What's the rush?'

'I've got some drawing to do.'

'Ah,' he said.

Maybe he didn't really understand the urgency of it, but he was an artist too, wasn't he? Though sculpture was more of a gradual process, she supposed.

'I'll give the dogs some water,' he said when they got home. 'You'd better get on with it.'

She still had the image in her mind, but it wasn't until she'd committed it to paper that she began to think about it properly.

What if Paul hadn't been silly enough to have forgotten about the incoming tide and wandered out on to the causeway? Even when drunk she didn't think that would have been like him. Had he wanted to get to the island for some reason? As far as she knew there was nothing there that would have tempted him. It had been close to Christmas and much too cold for there to have been an all-night party out there, or people camping.

The idea of him having been moved there after his death seemed more likely. Maybe somebody had accidentally or even deliberately killed him and then panicked and taken his body to the nearest place where the death might conceivably have been his own fault, or at the very least a complete accident. But wouldn't the police have known whether he'd drowned or met his death some other way? And how would anybody get the body on to the causeway? If the tide had been out at the time, somebody else could have tripped over it as they returned from the island – although what if it had already been pitch-black by then? The few street lights at the Cramond side wouldn't have been bright enough to illuminate dark deeds on the causeway.

If the tide had been well in before he'd been placed there, how had anybody got to the spot? Would it be possible to reach the causeway by boat at high tide? Pamela resolved to return at a time when she knew the tide would be low, and see how the land lay.

How could anybody be sure that the body wouldn't float away and wash up in the wrong place? Would that matter? The police hadn't said much about the position Paul had been found in. Was it possible to wedge something between the rocks or the upright posts in such a way that it wouldn't shift with the incoming tide?

Once again there were too many questions and not enough answers.

She glanced down at the sheets of paper littering her desk. Without really intending it, she had made a kind of comic strip out of her various ideas. In one frame, a mysterious killer in a dark mask wielded a knife to stab at Paul in an alley somewhere, in the next he rowed a boat over to the place where the posts stuck up out of the water like the bones of some massive prehistoric creature, marking the route of the causeway, and in the final one he had stuffed the body into a gap between the posts and was sailing away from the scene of the crime. She had even given the boat a little flag with a skull and crossbones on it. Dear God! What did it all say about the state of her subconscious?

Pamela was still staring at her work in horror when Andy knocked at the studio door to announce the arrival of coffee and biscuits.

She was too slow to hide the evidence. He stared in surprise for a moment and then said,

'Great! Have you ever done any animation?'

'No – I don't have the technical skills for it… Anyway, this kind of thing isn't meant for anybody else to see. I was just doodling.'

'Doodling? You should go into graphic novels. They're a big thing now.'

'Are they? I wouldn't want to publish this, though. It's too personal. I'll have to destroy them before the police come round again, too.'

'Anything goes if you fictionalise it,' said Andy.

'Fictionalise?'

'It's a word. I heard it at college.'

'Not in the English class, I hope,' she said primly.

'Do you really think somebody killed him?' he asked, looking again at the first of her frames.

'I have no idea,' said Pamela.

She hadn't told him what the police had said earlier, but she supposed she had better mention it now. They must have assumed she would pass it on to him.

'The police are considering whether to open a murder investigation,' she said. 'Apparently Paul might have been involved with criminals in some way, and I suppose anything like that's liable to end in violence.'

Andy took in this information without even blinking.

'I suppose it is,' he said after a moment's pause. 'What kind of criminals? Was it to do with his jewellery work?'

She nodded.

'I guess that was why we had to leave Glasgow, then,' he said slowly. 'I didn't say anything about it before, because I didn't want to worry you, but we left in a bit of a hurry.'

'Didn't you say something about men coming to the door?'

'That was after we moved here. There was that one time – did I tell you? – when they said it was Dad's last chance.'

'Yes, I remember.'

'Do you think it was the same people and they'd tracked him down?' said Andy. 'Or maybe it was to do with something completely different.'

'It seems like too much of a coincidence,' said Pamela. 'Did you say whether either of the men had anything to do with Caitlin French?'

'Caitlin? She was Mum's friend. What made you think of her?'

'I don't know,' said Pamela. 'She seems to have some quite dodgy acquaintances. Oh – and she gave me your old phone back. Sorry, I forgot to say. I had to hand it over to the police, but I suppose they'll give it back eventually. I really am sorry. Maybe you had contacts on it, photos, I don't know what people keep on their phones these days.'

'I'd like it back some time,' said Andy. 'The photos were backed up but I'd quite like the contacts. In case I missed anybody when I was setting up the new one.'

'I can't believe I forgot to tell you.'

'You've got a lot on your mind,' he said sombrely.

'Anyway,' Pamela went on, 'I told the police about finding the bag of gemstones in the box. I gave them it. At least they'll have somebody who can work out whether the things are real or not… They asked if Paul ever gave me jewellery. I suppose it's just as well he didn't, under the circumstances.'

'Mum had some, but it disappeared,' said Andy.

Pamela didn't know what to think now about the jewellery. On the one hand, she supposed she should be grateful to Paul for not palming off stolen goods on her. On the other, she couldn't help feeling a little resentful about him giving things to Joanne that he would never have dreamt of giving her.

'What's all this with the boat?' he asked.

'I was thinking about how somebody else could have moved Paul to the causeway if he – didn't walk on to it himself, and I wondered how close a boat could get.'

'It's maybe not deep enough for that, even with the tide in,' said Andy. 'One of these inflatables the lifeboat people use might work, though.'

It almost sounded as if he'd been thinking about the possibility too. Maybe she shouldn't be burdening him with all this, what with his exams and everything else. Losing both parents was more than enough for a boy of his age to worry about. On the other hand, he might feel even worse in the long run if he never knew the reason for it – if there was indeed a reason and neither death had been accidental.

'The police will know the answer to that too. If they've even thought of asking the question.'

Pamela wished she had somebody to ask. Iris had said she and Derek had a boat on the river at Cramond, but she was extremely reluctant to interact with either of them again, even in a good cause.

Should she mention to Detective Chief Inspector Mitchell the idea that an unknown killer had used a boat, or would he and his team already have considered it?

'We could try googling it,' suggested Andy.

Pamela didn't often resort to the internet for answers. In her experience there was too much misinformation there, and it could be very hard to distinguish between people who knew what they were talking about and others who just liked to talk. But she thought Andy would like something useful to do in the intervals of studying for his exams, and this might be a relatively harmless pastime.

'You might have a go,' she said. 'I'd better get on with some real work before I start to get nagging emails.'

Andy went away to make a start on it, while she resolutely stuffed the afternoon's sketches into a drawer so that they didn't distract her, and checked her calendar for the date of the next deadline.

Chapter 21 Eleanor Resurfaces

Pamela found herself driving round to Silverknowes with the dogs in mid-morning a couple of days after the expedition to the river mouth and the causeway at Cramond. She had dropped Andy off for his maths exam earlier, and she needed to do something, because she felt so nervous on his behalf. With luck she wouldn't see any of the people she'd previously encountered on the promenade, but she had no wish to give the dogs a bath again any time soon after an unfortunate incident in the woods the day before. Who knew there would be a marshy area halfway round a favoured dog walk? She hadn't realised Tiger would enjoy wallowing in it either. Or that he would somehow manage to cover not just the car interior but Lily with mud on the way home.

No doubt Eleanor Sharp would know a way of preventing dogs from wallowing in mud, if only Pamela could bring herself to consult the woman.

They walked some way along in the opposite direction from Cramond and the causeway, and then, somewhat concerned about the emptiness of the place that day, she turned back, thinking she might treat herself to a hot chocolate at the café. It did seem self-indulgent, as she had plenty of hot chocolate at home and it was only minutes away, but it was a harmless little treat too.

It must have been because of the promise of hot chocolate that she didn't react quickly enough when Tiger gave an extra strong tug on his lead, the clip came undone and he scampered off ahead of Pamela and Lily at a great rate.

Damn! Pamela bent and picked up Lily, whom she knew would object to being dragged along any faster than she had decided to go, which was never very fast. Panic, and the extra weight of the dog, which could not be more than a few pounds in truth, slowed her down as she came round the bend in the path and saw Tiger just passing the café ahead of them.

He was on his way up the slope when he paused to greet a woman who was approaching, and she grabbed him, hauling him up into her arms even as she held on to her own dog, a slightly larger terrier.

Oh, no! She must have conjured up Eleanor Sharp just by thinking of her.

Eleanor Sharp waved to her.

Pamela ran a little faster, which meant she was completely out of breath and probably extremely dishevelled, by the time she reached the woman. Not that the dishevelment mattered too much under the circumstances. She guessed Eleanor Sharp must have seen plenty of dishevelled dog-walkers in her time. It was more or less par for the course – not that Pamela was a golfer any more than she was a dog wrangler.

'Here we are,' said Eleanor. She had one hand at an awkward angle, and to Pamela's horror blood dripped from it on to the path.

'He didn't bite you?'

Eleanor laughed. 'Oh God, no! I wouldn't let that happen. No, there was something sharp…Well, would you look at that?'

She gently smoothed Tiger's fur away from his collar. There was a jagged piece of what looked like glass sticking out of it. Pamela had noticed the collar was studded with fake gems, but not that one was broken.

She quickly deposited Lily on the ground and looked for the collar catch. Her fingers fumbled, but at last it came undone and she lifted it off him. If the dog were hurt too….

'I'm so sorry,' she said. 'I had no idea… he isn't hurt, is he?'

'He's fine,' said Eleanor, handing over the dog. She fished in a pocket and produced a packet of wet wipes and a small box of plasters. 'Maybe I'd better sit down for a minute and sort this out.'

'Yes, of course! Will we have a hot drink? I know I could do with something.'

'Neat whisky would be more like the thing,' said Eleanor briskly, leading the way to the nearest table.

'Thank you for catching him,' said Pamela breathlessly. 'He managed to get the clip on his lead to undo. Goodness knows how that happened.'

'It'll have come a bit loose,' said Eleanor. 'Sometimes you can fix it, but you'll maybe have to buy a new lead. I would think about some kind of harness, if I were you, instead of the collars. Nothing too heavy – they're only wee dogs – but something secure. There are some kinds you can use in the car too.'

Eleanor showed her a temporary fix to make an improvised collar out of Tiger's lead and they tied up all three dogs.

'Having a tricky time?' she asked kindly once Pamela had brought out the drinks, along with blueberry muffins to help them over the shock.

'Don't ask!' said Pamela, responding to the polite question – which might not really have been a question at all, only for some reason she had the urge to answer it. She stared down at the collar that lay on the table between them. There was something about it that bothered her. She frowned.

'Silly kind of collar,' Eleanor remarked. 'I suppose it came with the dogs.'

'Lily has a different one – without the fake jewels,' said Pamela absently.

'You should put that one straight in the bin when you get home, otherwise somebody else is going to do themselves an injury.'

Fake jewels… Could somebody have imagined they were real? Was that what the dog thief had really been after? Paul's secret stash…

She glanced over at Eleanor again, meeting the other woman's clever brown eyes with the realisation that she desperately wanted to confide in her. She couldn't tell her everything, of course, but maybe it would help to share some of it.

'I've never understood why they even make collars like that,' said Eleanor.

'I didn't know they did, until I saw that one,' said Pamela. 'I wondered if somebody had stuck the jewels on after they'd bought it, for decoration.'

Or to hide stolen jewels, she thought. She gave a cough. Maybe she shouldn't say anything after all.

'I don't know why anybody would go to all that bother,' said Eleanor.

'My late husband was a jewellery designer,' said Pamela. She glanced round to make sure nobody was listening. The place was unusually deserted, however. She lowered her voice anyway. 'He was found dead on the causeway – halfway to Cramond Island. The police are saying he got mixed up with the wrong crowd… Sorry, that sounds a bit dramatic.'

'Those things happen,' said Eleanor in a tone that suggested she'd seen it all before, although Pamela was willing to bet that she hadn't. Not quite like this, anyway.

'He had a second wife and family, and I only ever knew about the designing part. Not all the other stuff about possible jewel theft. He would have been able to melt down pieces of jewellery and re-use the gems in other settings, you see.'

Eleanor blinked. 'I'm not sure you should be telling me all this, but do go on. It's fascinating.'

Once she had started, Pamela found it impossible to stop. It all came out, although maybe not in any sensible order. Eleanor made her pause once or twice and explain something. But in the end there it all was. On the table, along with Tiger's discarded collar and the muffin wrappers and the empty mugs.

'The police don't suspect you of being involved, do they?'

There was a note of disbelief in her voice that almost made Pamela laugh. She must indeed seem too naïve and trusting to have willingly taken part in anything like this. Why had she never questioned Paul's inability to get away from work during the week, even for events he would once have cut off his own arm rather than miss, like the prestigious jewellery event at one of the Edinburgh galleries? Never taking a holiday was a little easier to understand. He had always been too immersed in his work to want a break for any reason. She had resorted in past years to going away somewhere with her mother. She found herself resenting him even now for the fact that she had almost forgotten to mourn her mother because his death had loomed larger than anything else.

'I don't think I'm a suspect,' she told Eleanor. 'They won't have far to go to catch up with me if they need to, anyway. The Chief Inspector lives next-door to me.'

'Mal Mitchell? Oh, that's all right then.'

'Do you know him?'

'We're old adversaries,' said Eleanor with relish.

That didn't sound very helpful. Surely the other woman must be joking.

'It's Andy I'm most worried about,' Pamela went on. 'He's in the middle of his exams at the moment.'

'Andy?'

'Andy Hutchison. He was the one who gave me the dogs in the first place. They'd belonged to his family – his parents were my late husband and his other wife. I've sort of adopted him now.'

'So you're a kind of stepmother? But not the wicked kind, obviously.'

'I hope not.'

'Dear me,' said Eleanor. 'So your life's more complicated now than it was a few weeks ago. No wonder you gave me that look when I suggested dog training classes!'

'Sorry,' said Pamela, wondering what sort of look she might have given the woman at their first meeting. 'I can see why I need the classes. Only I'll have to wait until at least some of this mess gets cleared up before I start on anything else.'

'That's not a problem. Have you still got my card, or did you tear it up and throw it in the bin when you got home last time?' Eleanor got up from the table as she spoke. 'I'd better get going – I've got a few appointments later.'

'It's still in my pocket, don't worry… Thank you for listening. I wasn't asking for help – it was just that my mind was overflowing with thoughts and some of them spilled out.'

'Please, don't apologise. And don't concern yourself that I will pass any of it on. If you need any help, with the dogs or anything else, do get in touch.'

'Thank you.'

They parted company at the top of the slope. Pamela didn't exactly feel as if a weight had been lifted off her, but she did feel obscurely more able to bear it after speaking to Eleanor. She thought the other woman could become a friend at some point in the future, once all this was over with.

She had no idea how far ahead that point might be, but she was convinced there must be a resolution eventually.

Chapter 22 Results

Andy's maths exam didn't sound as if it had gone too badly, which was one good thing that came out of the day. It was slightly overshadowed, in Pamela's mind anyway, by her latest anxiety about whether she'd been wrong to confide in Eleanor, who was after all almost a stranger. Still, if you had to confide in a stranger, then a vet was probably a good choice for it, since they must see people at their best and worst when dealing with sick and dying animals.

And overfed ones, Pamela reminded herself as she gave the dogs a few treats to make up to Tiger for making him wear an unsuitable collar and lead. Not that she had given him them, of course.

She asked Andy if he thought the some of the jewels on the collar might be real gemstones, and he just laughed.

'I'll go to the pet shop tomorrow if you like, and get him a replacement,' he offered. 'I've got the day off from college. Nothing better to do.'

'Haven't you got more revision to be going on with?'

He gave her an odd look, and she hastily backtracked.

'It's up to you, though. I expect you've got it all planned out.'

'Sure I have,' he said.

He was out at the pet shop the following day when Detective Chief Inspector Mitchell re-appeared. Pamela was trying hard to think of him by his official title and not merely by his name as Eleanor had referred to him. It would be nice, she thought, to be able to relax enough to drop the title, if they ever got through all this and out the other side.

He had brought the woman officer with him again, though she seemed to be a kind of silent partner. Pamela wondered if she ever got a word in edgeways among all the men she worked with. Still, she supposed some women rose to great heights in the police so they must have their say sometimes.

'I'm afraid I have something fairly grim to tell you, Mrs Prendergast,' said Mitchell after they had all sat down. 'I can only apologise that none of us spotted it sooner. Once we started looking for it, we noticed it quite quickly.'

Pamela willed herself not to faint or have hysterics or say anything silly. She couldn't remember doing any of these things when the police had first brought her the news of Paul's death, but you never knew when the cumulative effect of everything might suddenly become too much to bear.

'That's all right,' she said quietly. 'I suppose when you find somebody in the water you assume they drowned.'

'We shouldn't ever assume,' he said. 'We try not to. In fact the boys in the path lab said something about this but it got lost in translation. That's no excuse, though.'

He took a deep breath before going on.

'I'm we now have reason to believe Mr Prendergast may have been killed deliberately, but it took place while he was actually in the water, so the signs were similar to those of a natural death by drowning.'

'In the water?'

He nodded. 'The lungs had salt water in them, just as you might expect in the Firth of Forth, but there were marks on his arms suggesting he might have been held or tied down. We previously believed the marks must have been the result of some contact with the concrete posts alongside the causeway as the tide got higher – as if he had been thrown back and forwards repeatedly by the action of the water. However when the lab revisited the photographs, they came up with at least two more possible explanations.'

He'd been watching her closely as he spoke, perhaps to make sure she was taking the news well, which she was. His eyes were dark and deep-set. Fathoms deep, she thought, while knowing she had made the connection as a way of distracting herself from what he was saying. The frames of a movie featuring Paul being held down as the water covered him, of his last frantic struggles until he finally gave up and let himself be overwhelmed, played in her mind. She wouldn't be turning this into a comic book, that was for sure, except in her nightmares.

'Were the people who did this to him in a boat, then?'

'We believe they were likely to have been in some kind of a vessel. It might have been similar to some of the inflatables used by lifeboat crews, with very little draught. Or even a small rowing-boat.'

'Yes,' she said.

'There are several rowing-boats moored in the harbour. We're making further enquiries.'

'Thank you,' she said.

She was definitely not going to faint or go into hysterics, but she would very much like the opportunity to curl up in a ball like a hedgehog and not have to speak to anybody for some time. Except that Andy would be back from the pet shop soon, and the dogs would need feeding, and...

'Are you all right, Mrs Prendergast?' said the woman officer suddenly. 'Can I get you a glass of water or something?'

Pamela sighed. 'I don't really drink water,' she said. 'Don't worry, I'll be fine.'

'The boy lives with you at the moment, doesn't he?' said the Chief Inspector. 'Is he here now?'

'He's gone to the pet shop for something,' Pamela told him. 'Tiger needs a new collar and lead.'

'Of course. The dogs belonged to the Hutchisons. Do you plan to keep them now?'

'Oh yes, I think so. Andy won't want the responsibility. He's been staying in a bedsit over towards the college – I doubt if the landlady would welcome them there... I quite like having them around anyway.'

'Good,' he said. 'They'll be great company. There's nothing like having a dog around for the company.'

He looked rather sad suddenly. Pamela wondered if he had recently lost a pet. Maybe that was the connection between him and Eleanor.

'Tiger's collar had glass beads stuck round it. One of them got broken somehow. That's why he needs a new one.'

'Glass beads?' said the Chief Inspector. 'That's getting to be a bit of a theme, isn't it? By the way, we think the gemstones you gave me are real ones, but that's still to be finally confirmed.'

'I wonder where they came from,' said Pamela.

She was really wondering whether the stones had been in Paul's possession as the result of a crime, but she was oddly reluctant to come out and ask the detective directly.

He gave her an enigmatic look.

'Possibly the proceeds of crime, but we can't possibly tell just yet. If we can establish they were obtained through legal means, we will of course return them to you.'

'Yes,' she said, 'of course.'

She heard the click of a key in the front door lock, and then footsteps in the hall. Thank heaven it couldn't be Iris or Derek, now that she had taken the key away from them. Unless they'd made a copy, of course. She wouldn't be entirely surprised to find that was the case.

The door to the front room opened a little way.

'Mrs Prendergast? I've got the collar and lead. Do you want to try them on Tiger right away?'

'I'll be out in a minute,' she said. 'I've got Mr Mitchell here. And another police officer – sorry I didn't catch your name,' she added to the woman officer, feeling guilty that she hadn't taken more notice.

'I'll leave them in the kitchen for you,' said Andy from outside the room.

She wasn't surprised that he didn't want to come in and meet the two police officers. He'd probably seen enough of them already.

But on the way out, the chief inspector took a few steps towards the kitchen and spoke to Andy, and they exchanged a few sentences that Pamela couldn't hear. She and the woman officer had also chatted for a minute or two, and now she was confident of remembering the woman's name the next time they met. Linda Cameron. She repeated it to herself once the police had gone.

'What was that?' said Andy.

'I was just memorising the woman's name. I felt guilty for not paying attention.'

'Doesn't take much, does it?' he muttered. He had wrangled the new collar on to Tiger. This one was in Royal Stewart tartan without any jewellery.

'What?'

He smiled. 'To make you feel guilty.... What do you think of it?' he added. 'I've got one for Lily too, but you'll have to catch her for me to put it on..'

'It's very smart. Does the lead match it?'

He nodded. 'I thought it was a bit classy.'

'I don't care whether it's classy or not, as long as it does what it's meant to do,' said Pamela, remembering the scare she'd had when Tiger had pulled away from her and had gone running on ahead towards the road at the top of the slope. 'Thanks for going for all of it, though.'

'There's some dog treats in the bag too.' He gestured towards a carrier bag on the worktop. 'They're special ones for small breeds of dog... What did the police want this time?'

'We'd better have a coffee,' she said.

'As bad as that?'

She nodded.

Once they were sitting at the table again with their coffee mugs and a medicinal packet of biscuits between them, she told him what the police had said.

'So Dad was murdered, then?' he asked at the end of her account.

'They still don't know that for sure. It's just that they're considering it as a possibility, in the light of re-examining the evidence, and what they now know about the background.'

'About his double life, you mean.'

'And they've revisited the photographs and crime scene reports.'

Andy's expression was sombre.

'They think the gemstones we found may be real, too,' she added. 'But they might be able to give them back to us if they can't link them to any crimes.'

'Big deal.'

'Yes, I know.'

'Still, he brought it all on himself,' said Andy. 'You'd think being able to make a living doing what he wanted to do would have been enough. He didn't have to go into crime just to get more money.'

Pamela laughed despite herself. 'Maybe he thought he needed more to support his double life.'

'Well, yes,' said Andy. He glanced across at her. 'You don't seem to be bitter about it.'

'I'm not bitter about you and your Mum,' she said. 'I suppose if I'd found out at the time, I might have been angrier. As it is, I don't know, but I can't reduce this whole thing to me feeling bitter. There's too much of it to process. And we don't know the whole story yet. We maybe never will.'

She patted his hand, hoping he wouldn't whisk it away in disgust. 'I'm glad to have got to know you, anyway.'

'Oh, please,' he said, though he was smiling. 'This is turning into one of those Christmas movies.'

'We'll be lucky if it doesn't turn out to have been made by Hitchcock,' she muttered.

Chapter 23 Walking with Yorkies

Just as Pamela was hoping to get on with some work the next morning, ahead of her next deadline, the phone rang.

'Surprise!' said Kim brightly.

'Hello! How are you getting on with the new romance?'

'Don't ask,' said Kim. 'We weren't compatible. But hey, just as well I found out before it was too late. How's your sexy policeman?'

'Kim! How old are you? I didn't say he was sexy, anyway!'

Kim giggled.

'He's got to be. There wouldn't be much of a story otherwise. And don't make me think about how old I am.'

'I'm already living in a story, but I'm afraid it's a bit darker than that,' said Pamela.

'Tell me everything! I'm only up at the shops by the traffic lights – I can be with you in five minutes.'

Pamela laughed. 'What are you doing there? And don't tell me you happened to be passing.'

'It's a long story. I'll bring refreshments.'

Kim was on the door-step seven minutes later, bearing a bag of assorted highly coloured cakes as well as an ominous-looking weekend case, and looking as bright as she had sounded on the phone.

'There! All we need is coffee to go with these.'

'We'll have to walk them off afterwards,' Pamela warned her. 'The dogs have been waiting for their exercise.'

'That's fine – we can go and parade along the prom like – what kind of people walk along the prom? Edwardians?'

Pamela laughed. 'Mostly dog people in beige waterproof jackets around here. Not nearly as elegant.'

'Where are the wee dogs, then? And what about your house-guest?'

'Andy's gone out to speak to his college tutor, and I shut the dogs in the kitchen while I tried to get some work done.'

'Sorry to interrupt,' said Kim in a not-sorry tone.

'I thrive on interruptions,' said Pamela, although she was certain the people employing her to illustrate the latest baby animal book would agree.

'He was driving me back from a few days in the Highlands,' Kim explained while they demolished the cakes. 'I asked him to let me off at the traffic lights. We were hardly speaking by then anyway. Can you believe we were in a romantic cottage miles from anywhere and he actually wanted to drive to the pub just to watch some obscure football match? Of course I had to put my foot down about that. But he grumbled about it all the next day, when we were touring a couple of castles and a distillery… I knew he wasn't my type when he wouldn't go up to the top of the towers in either of the castles, and he claimed not to like whisky and sat outside in the car waiting for me, and then complained about me having had just the tiniest nip of it.'

Ah. That explained the weekend case, currently sitting near the front door. Pamela had witnessed Kim having the tiniest nip of whisky before. She wasn't entirely unsympathetic to the discarded man's point of view about that. Still, Kim was one of her oldest friends and the experience must have hurt a little. She made a few remarks she hoped were soothing, and listened a bit more, and then raised the topic of walking the dogs again.

'I won't be able to go anywhere too wild in those shoes,' Kim pointed out. 'And I'm not dressed for dog-walking. Unless you've got a spare beige jacket I can borrow?'

'The prom has a good surface, and it's flat. There's only the slope to get down to it from the place where I park the car. And it isn't going to rain. You don't need a beige jacket.'

'I should just about manage, then. Let's go now before we lose the urge.'

The dogs, resplendent in their tartan collars, were beside themselves with excitement about having Kim in the car with them. Pamela felt she should have given them a stern lecture on the topic of not trying to run off before going out, only Kim would probably have thought she was losing her grip.

If only they didn't encounter Caitlin French, they'd be fine.

'Can we go that way?' said Kim once they reached the promenade. She had seen Cramond Island in the middle distance. 'I've never been to the island. You can get there at low tide, can't you?'

She peered at the shore, presumably to try and estimate the state of the tide.

'That was where Paul died,' said Pamela flatly.

She didn't want to visit the causeway with somebody like Kim, who would ask for exhaustive details and maybe dissolve into fake emotion, which would be unbearable.

'Really? Oh, sorry, I didn't know that. Don't tell me any more unless you want to.'

Pamela immediately felt guilty. Obviously her friend knew when not to pry into something.

'It's all right – I just don't think I'm ready to go there yet. Maybe next time you're here.'

'Yes, next time,' said Kim. 'We'd better head along the other way for now – does it go anywhere interesting?'

'I don't know but I think it just comes out on another road. Though maybe you can walk all the way to Leith if you're feeling very energetic.'

'I doubt if I'll make it that far,' said Kim cheerfully. 'It's lovely being able to look out over the Forth, anyway... Look at that white ship – over there in the middle. Do you think that's one of the cruise ships?'

They chatted amicably, planning exotic and completely imaginary holidays in faraway places, as they went along. Pamela wasn't planning to let the dogs off the lead today. She knew she wouldn't be able to keep an eye on them while still listening to Kim. With luck they wouldn't encounter Eleanor this time. She might disapprove of the two of them using the dog walk as a social event. Though Pamela had seen plenty of dog-walkers who obviously did just that, without any apparent ill-effects for the dogs.

After walking a little further than Pamela usually managed on her own, they turned back towards their starting-point. There were still only a few other people about, mostly on foot, but a couple of bikes swooped past them on the way, and once a car with a park ranger logo on it came along, much more slowly than the bikes.

This must be a quiet time. Pamela didn't know whether to be glad about that or not. It was just as well she had brought Kim with her, though. At least there would be a witness if anything awful happened. But they reached the slope where they would follow the path up to the road and the sanctuary of the car, without incident.

Almost as soon as the thought crossed her mind, she saw a man step out on to the path ahead of them, about halfway up the slope. He must have been lurking by the wall that ran along by the road in places, or maybe even hiding behind it and lying in wait for them, which was an even more uncomfortable idea. It was obvious immediately that he had a large dog with him, one of the kind that had a squashed-in face like a pugilist who had had his nose broken once too often. The man's stance, squarely in the middle of the path, and the dog's features, caused alarm bells to ring in Pamela's mind.

She picked up Lily and grabbed Kim's arm.

'Let's go another way.'

'Why?' said Kim.

'I don't think we should go past that man... His dog might scare those two.'

'Just because the dog has an ugly face doesn't mean he'll attack us,' Kim protested, pulling her arm away and marching on.

'No – Kim. Wait.'

The man and dog took a couple of steps downwards. Pamela recognised the man now. He was the same pallid, puffy-faced man whom she had last seen with Caitlin French. Maybe they were partners. Or partners in crime, at least. The dog wasn't Caitlin's dog, however. It had been smaller and a lot less ugly.

'Kim,' she said more urgently still.

Kim glanced back over her shoulder. 'Hurry up, we just need to get to the car before we both freeze to death.'

'It isn't nearly cold enough for that. Let's go round the other way.'

Kim had almost reached the man and dog. Pamela speeded up a bit, trying to overcome the instincts that screamed at her to retreat. She couldn't let her friend walk into a trap like this… But Kim simply walked past the danger point, and started beckoning from further up the path. She must think Pamela was an idiot to have panicked.

The man and his dog moved a little further down the path.

They were only about ten steps away from Pamela when he bent and unclipped his dog's lead from the collar, and the animal sprang forward. Pamela only had seconds to decide what to do. Still holding Lily in her arms and dragging a reluctant Tiger, who, she now realised, had been eyeing the other dog with extreme suspicion, behind her, she stepped off the path on to the grassy slope beside it.

Of course, she recalled as her foot slipped and she began to fall, it had rained again overnight and the grass was wet and there weren't any footholds.

She twisted while still falling, to avoid crushing Lily beneath her, but she felt the almost indiscernible weight of the little dog leave her just before she hit the ground. She hoped Lily had leapt to safety and that Tiger had also got out of the way, but she found she had closed her eyes, perhaps hoping not to see any squashed Yorkies.

Something licked her ear. She opened her eyes to see that it wasn't one of her own dogs but the one with the unprepossessing features. Goodness knows where that tongue had been. She heaved herself up to a sitting position, wincing from the effort and breathless from residual panic. The dog ran off.

'Kindly control your dog!' somebody snapped from further down the slope.

'... not doing any harm,' said a man's voice. '... wasn't my fault.'

'Just do it, before he causes any more accidents,' said the first voice, a woman. Eleanor! Where had she come from?

'Pamela!' gasped Kim, running towards her.

'Slow down,' Pamela told her. 'And don't set foot on the grass – it's slippery.'

Kim did as she was told, for once, but she got hold of Tiger's lead and looked for Lily.

'It's all right, I've got her,' said the woman's voice from somewhere below them.

Pamela glanced in that direction. Eleanor had tucked Lily under her arm and was approaching, her own dog on the lead walking sedately just ahead of her. There was no sign of the pale man and the ugly dog. They must have beaten a hasty retreat after being admonished by Eleanor.

'Well, that was an ugly-looking brute,' said Eleanor as she got nearer. She gazed at Pamela, who was still sitting on the damp grass. 'Do you need a hand to get up?'

'Give me a minute or two,' said Pamela. 'Are the dogs all right?'

'All present and correct,' said Eleanor. 'The other one's nice enough natured. He just looks a bit fierce.'

'Do you know him, then?' Pamela asked.

'He's a patient of mine. I don't see him very often, mind you. The owner doesn't believe in regular vaccinations or check-ups. But then, the owner's a different kettle of fish from his dog. I wouldn't want to meet him in a dark alley.'

'I've seen him before,' said Pamela. 'With Caitlin French.'

'Really?' said Eleanor. 'I'd have thought she had more sense. Still, there's no telling some people.'

'Are you allowed to tell me his name?' Pamela asked. 'Or is it covered by patient confidentiality?'

'He isn't exactly my patient,' said Eleanor.

Kim and Tiger had been waiting as this conversation took place. Pamela realised Kim must be wondering what was going on. She introduced the women to each other and thanked her friend for looking after Tiger.

'I think I'm ready to get up now,' she said after pleasantries had been exchanged. 'As long as I don't rush it, I should be fine.'

'Does anything hurt?' asked Eleanor. 'Can you feel all your limbs?'

Pamela nodded. 'I might have some colourful bruises, though.'

Between them, Kim and Eleanor got Pamela back on her feet, and on to the relative safety of the path.

'What was he like when you met him before?' Eleanor asked.

By common consent they'd retired to the café for medicinal hot drinks. This was getting to be a routine development.

'Who? The man with the dog? He was a bit threatening that time, I thought, but only in a very obscure kind of way.'

Eleanor shook her head. 'If you hadn't taken matters into your own hands – or feet – and slipped, he might easily have done something today. Still, with Kim here he wouldn't want to make
an obvious move. It might be better if you brought the boy – Andy – here with you in future.'

'I suppose so,' said Pamela, and sighed. 'It makes me feel as if I'm not fit to be out on my own. I thought I might have another twenty or so years left before I got to that stage.'

Kim patted her hand. 'You might still have that long. You just need to get the sexy detective on the case.'

'Sexy detective?' said Eleanor. 'Am I missing something?' She looked from Kim to Pamela and back again. 'Not Mal Mitchell?'

She started to laugh – rather loudly and raucously. The people at the next table but one turned and stared.

'It's Kim's phrase for him, not mine,' muttered Pamela. 'She hasn't even met him.'

'Don't worry, I won't tell him,' said Eleanor, recovering. 'We aren't on those kind of terms… Mind you, I suppose there is something quite sexy about his eyes – in certain lights. But don't you ever tell him that, either.'

After they'd finished their hot drinks, Eleanor inspected the new collars and leads and gave them her seal of approval, although she repeated her advice about finding harnesses for the two little dogs.

'They're a bit more secure than collars – maybe more comfortable too, although that may depend on how much the dog pulls. Better to train them not to. You might be able to clip them on to seat-belts too. Do they behave themselves in the car? I've known dogs to get completely over-excited if they think they're going for a walk, even after the hundredth time. Memories like goldfish, some of them.'

'Thanks,' said Pamela. 'I'd better get them checked over before long. I wouldn't want you to think I'm only open to advice if I don't want to pay for it.'

'I'm sure you're not one of those people,' said Eleanor.

On that friendly note they parted company.

'Handy to have a vet and a policeman at your beck and call,' remarked Kim on the drive home.

'Mr Mitchell isn't exactly at my beck and call. Neither is Eleanor for that matter. She's more of a friend, at least I hope she is.'

'Do you think people are friendlier here than in the New Town?'

Pamela considered this for a moment before replying.

'I'm not sure. It's partly the different circumstances, I think. Maybe the New Town would have seemed friendlier if I'd had the dogs then.'

'Or maybe more hostile,' Kim suggested. 'People complaining about them barking or something.'

Andy was in the kitchen when they got back to the bungalow, so she had to introduce them to each other. She wasn't at all sure they would get along, but when she took Kim into the studio to show her the latest efforts, he trailed along after them.

'Have you shown Kim your comic strip?' he said. 'It's very cool.'

'It isn't really for anybody to see,' said Pamela. 'It isn't finished,' she added, for Kim's benefit. 'Andy only saw it by accident – I don't usually show people anything until it's finished.'

'I know you don't,' said Kim. 'All right, what was the last thing you actually completed?'

'I did a sketch of Andy,' said Pamela.

Andy groaned. 'Oh, please.'

He turned away when Pamela got out the sketch. Kim studied it for a couple of minutes.

'It certainly brings out the likeness,' she said. 'Don't you think?'

Pamela stared at the sketch, wondering if Andy was as like Paul as the version of him that she had drawn, or whether her memories of Paul had somehow permeated the whole thing so that it was an amalgam of both of them.

Impossible to tell.

'Yes, I suppose it does,' she said vaguely, still staring at it.

Later, she offered to drive Kim home, but her friend claimed she would prefer to go by bus. Later still, Pamela realised she hadn't put the car away in the garage, despite the advice from the police officers who had visited her recently. Still, she would probably want to use it in the morning,
and she was really too tired after the events of the day to make the effort. The chances of anything happening to it were surely very small indeed.

Chapter 24 Panic on the Coast Road

Pamela woke up the next morning with so many new aches and pains that she didn't know at first how she was going to get out of bed, never mind take the dogs out, but fortunately Andy was at home that day – the weekend had arrived without her noticing – and said he would walk them along to Lauriston Castle and back.

After half an hour or so when she hobbled around the house, feeling a good deal older than her actual age, Pamela decided she was at least capable of sitting at her desk and doing some long-postponed work there. By the time she'd finished off a couple of commissions that were fast approaching their deadline, and made a start on her email backlog, she realised it was nearly one o'clock and there had been no sign of Andy returning with the dogs.

Almost in the same moment, she heard the click of the front door opening, and the scurrying of small feet along the hall in the direction of the kitchen.

'Sorry we were so long,' Andy called through the half-open door.

Lily pushed it further open and rushed in to greet Pamela effusively.

'What would you like to eat?' Pamela enquired.

'Just now? I can get something, it's fine.'

'I need a break,' she said, stretching her arms and wiggling her fingers. 'There are still about nine million emails to get through. I can do egg on toast or something first.'

'Nine million?' said Andy, laughing.

'Just a rough estimate. Would you prefer soup?'

She reached the kitchen to find Tiger sitting by his empty dish. Lily immediately copied him, and they both gazed meltingly at her.

'Was everything all right when you were out?' said Pamela, not wanting to pry into why the walk had taken so long, but curious all the same.

'It was fine,' said Andy. He added, after a pause, 'We had to come back a different way, that was why we were so long.'

'I was so busy I didn't notice the time passing,' said Pamela truthfully.

'Yes – we were just going into the castle gardens when those two men came round the corner from that road that leads up from the roundabout by the golf course.'

'Two men? Oh, you mean the men who were chasing you the other day?'

Pamela paused in the act of pouring dog biscuits into the bowls, trying to divide them equally although Tiger always ate twice as much as Lily did. Some of the biscuits spilled on to the floor and Tiger scoffed them immediately.

'I think it was them again…. Anyway, we sneaked out at the back of the gardens and round by some paths to the shore and then along to Cramond harbour. It was maybe a bit too much for the dogs, though.'

'Just as well to keep out of the way of those men,' Pamela observed. She moved Lily's bowl to the other side of the kitchen and re-filled it. 'Even if they weren't looking for you, it was best not to come up against them.'

'I saw that nosy neighbour of yours again down at the harbour,' he added. 'Iris. She said she was getting the boat ready.'

'Maybe they're going to sail off into the sunset,' muttered Pamela. 'Fingers crossed.'

She would never have guessed, the first time she had met Iris, that the woman would be such an outdoor type. But it was possible Derek had been the one who enjoyed sailing, and also possible that they were preparing the boat to sell and not to go anywhere. She told herself not to get her hopes up.

The dogs curled up at her feet for much of the day as she worked. Andy seemed to have gone back to bed, but when she emerged from the studio she heard music from the direction of his room. Probably just chilling out, she thought.

On Sunday she had the idea of taking Andy and the dogs somewhere completely different, where they wouldn't run the risk of bumping into anybody they knew, whether it was Iris or Caitlin French and her friends and partners, or even Eleanor Sharp. She had a feeling Eleanor would probably prefer not to have to step in and rescue her again just yet either.

'What do you think?' she asked him when he surfaced for a late breakfast, which was probably more like a brunch. 'Portobello or maybe Gullane?'

He shrugged. 'Don't know. It's up to you.'

'Let's just get in the car and see what happens, then.'

In theory Pamela liked the idea of making up their minds as they went along, but in practice it turned out to be more problematic than expected.

For one thing, the car had acquired, apparently overnight, a tendency to veer towards the side of the road. At first she wondered if there was something odd about the road surface – you never knew, with Edinburgh roads, whether they were trying out some new-fangled method of repairing potholes – but after a while the tendency became even more pronounced and she pulled into a parking bay and got out to investigate.

The front tyre on the driver's side looked rather flat, and when she walked round to the passenger side she found the other front tyre was even worse.

'Damn!'

She was more annoyed with herself than with the tyres. Why hadn't she at least spared them a glance before she and Andy and the dogs had set off? In fact, she knew perfectly well why not – it was because she'd been concentrating on getting both dogs into the back seat without at least one of them escaping before she closed the door on them.

There followed a very trying couple of hours while they all waited for the rescue organisation, meanwhile twice having to fend off traffic wardens who tried to move them on.

The rescue man looked very serious when he had finished examining the faulty tyres.

'We're going to have to get you to a garage. Looks like there are holes in both those tyres, and you've got a couple of loose wheel-nuts too. Probably vandalism.'

'Vandalism?' said Pamela blankly.

He nodded. 'Happens all the time these days. You've likely parked in a dodgy neighbourhood. You'll need two new tyres.'

'Not really,' said Pamela, irked by the oblique accusation in his words. 'The car's been parked outside my house the last couple of nights.'

The man wasn't listening. 'I'll need to put you on a truck. It'll take a while.'

Andy had been listening to the verdict. 'I could take the dogs for a quick walk while we wait, if you want,' he said. 'Or I can wait with the car and you can walk them.'

'All right, but don't go too far away,' said Pamela. 'It sounds as if we might have to get a bus somewhere.'

'They'll only take one of you with them,' said the rescue man. 'And probably not the dogs.'

'Maybe you'd better take them home on the bus, then,' she told Andy. 'Give them a quick walk first – we're not far from the beach here. Or would you rather I called a taxi?'

Andy laughed. 'We'll be fine on the bus. I've done it before.'

'OK then,' said Pamela. 'I don't know how long I'll be.'

This was an inconvenience, she told herself, and nothing more than that. She pushed aside the idea of her car having been deliberately vandalised. Though she might speak to Iris about it later, assuming she could bring herself to set foot on the neighbours' doorstep again. Maybe Iris's warning hadn't been quite so random after all.

Much later, well into the evening. she wearily opened the garage door in order to put the car away safely inside. It was only laziness that had prevented her from doing so on all the other days since the move. She hadn't stored anything very much in the space, even temporarily. Most of her boxes had been in the room now occupied by Andy, so there was only the old sideboard against the back wall, and that was positioned there partly to stop the car from running into the wall if it somehow got away from her on the way into the garage.

Andy and the dogs already occupied the front room, where he had switched on the electric fire and the dogs were warming themselves on the rug in front of it.

'You don't mind me putting the heater on, do you?' he said anxiously. 'I thought the dogs might be cold… Is the car all right?'

'It's fine now. He was right, it did need two new tyres. And the wheel-nuts tightening up. The wheel-nut thing could have been more dangerous if we'd gone at any speed.'

'Just as well we didn't get any further without noticing, then,' he said.

'Have you eaten?'

'Not yet. Do you want me to get us something?'

'Let's order in again.'

Eating pizza from the coffee table in the cosiness of the front room – Pamela asked herself why she hadn't even thought of switching the heater on before this – she began to relax at last. She was still uneasy about the way these various minor incidents were adding up. What was the point of them? Was somebody trying to drive her away, or was the real intention to harm her? She couldn't really believe either of these theories. Did she have something they wanted? Without knowing who 'they' were, she couldn't provide an answer to that either, although it seemed just about feasible that the motive was still connected with Paul being in cahoots with a gang of jewel thieves, though she didn't think she had anything they wanted anyway.

But maybe they didn't know that.

She mulled over a few silly ideas such as putting a sign on the front door saying jewel thieves weren't welcome, in the same way that some people had signs designed to turn away door-to-door salesmen or religious missionaries or anybody trying to sell lucky white heather. Or maybe doing something like this on social media was the way to go these days, though that would probably only attract unwelcome attention and not deter anybody.

'A lot of things have been happening,' remarked Andy, intruding abruptly into her fantasy world.

'Yes, they have,' said Pamela. 'Do you get the feeling they're all connected?'

'I was wondering about that… Are you going to tell the police about Friday and today?'

'What happened on Friday could've been just my own silliness,' she said. 'I suppose the rescue people could back me up on what happened with the car, though.'

'You could just have a quick word with Chief Inspector Mitchell,' said Andy. 'He seems all right.'

'I expect he's got enough to deal with already, and I don't want to take up his time.'

'He's already investigating Dad's death, though, isn't he? What if this is all part of the same thing? If you keep it from him, then you'll get into trouble later when he finds out.'

She stared at him. 'I hadn't thought of it like that.'

Pamela hoped this wasn't the start of a downward decline into old age, when she would find that people much younger than her were suddenly far wiser. Or maybe it was just a one-off. A blip.

'I'll try and catch him in the morning,' she added. 'Is that soon enough?'

Chapter 25 Catching the Detective

Pamela didn't exactly want to lie in wait for Detective Chief Inspector Mitchell like some pathetic stalker, but neither did she think it worth calling him on the mobile number he'd given her. After all, she reasoned, he might be in the middle of a car chase or a hostage situation, in which case her car problems would be an unwelcome distraction to say the least.

Did Chief Inspectors take part in car chases? She supposed they must have to sometimes. She could imagine them negotiating the release of hostages on occasion too.

As it happened, she saw him when she took one of the wheelie-bins out to the kerb in the morning – she should have put it out the previous night but she hadn't quite got the hang of the bin collection schedule in her new home and had only realised it was recycling day when she saw Iris and Derek's bin. They were just the kind of people who had the bin calendar hard-wired into their brains, so she guessed it was safe to rely on them.

The detective inspector was just getting into his car, which contrary to received wisdom he seemed to have left in the drive overnight. She was willing to bet nobody would dare to slash his tyres or loosen his wheel-nuts.

He closed the door again and came over to speak to her.

'You look as if you have something to tell me,' he said.

'How did you guess? I just wanted to let you know, in case it turns out to be relevant, that my car was vandalised while it was parked in my drive. Two of the tyres were damaged and the wheel-nuts had been tampered with. I suppose I should have at least glanced at the tyres before we set out, but I didn't think of it. It isn't very long since I got two new ones, and so it really wasn't on my radar.'

'No need to apologise to me,' he said. 'As long as you're all right, which I can see you are… You're quite right to mention it, though.'

He paused, evidently thinking over this development.

'I noticed something was wrong and we stopped and called the rescue people,' Pamela added.

'Just as well you did,' he said. 'Have you got the car back now?'

'It's in my garage.'

'I wonder if we should send a team round to go over it, although if it's been in one of the tyre places there won't be much to find by now. In the way of evidence, I mean.'

'Sorry, I didn't think of that.'

'It's fine – I suppose you just wanted it back on the road. I'd leave it in your garage when you're not using it in future, if I were you. Though they may not be back to do any more damage. But be careful, particularly when you're walking those dogs of yours.'

'I fell over the other day when we were out. But that was just accidental,' she added hastily, not wanting to go into yet another minor incident.

'Tell me about it anyway,' he said. 'Come and sit in the car for a minute. It's too cold to be standing about here for long.'

She was surprised he had thought of that, or that he considered her accidental fall worth his notice.

Though of course Kim and Andy had both advised her to mention it to him.

They sat in his car, which was about twice the size of hers, and she explained about the fall.

'But it was really only the wet grass,' she concluded. 'I couldn't blame the dog, or even its owner.'

'But he was blocking your way, and that was why you stepped on to the grass?'

'Yes, but he couldn't have known I would fall over. It was just coincidence. And my friend was with me, though it maybe didn't look as if we were together. She'd got a bit ahead of me on the slope because Lily wouldn't get a move on. And then Eleanor Sharp – the vet – wasn't far away either.'

'So he wasn't to know you were with somebody… Had you seen him before? Did you recognise him at all?'

'I'd seen him with Caitlin before,' she said. 'But they weren't all that friendly. He's got a really ugly dog, and a kind of unhealthy-looking face.'

'Mmhm,' he said. 'I think it's about time we had a word with Alan French.'

'You know who he is?'

'Oh, yes. We've been keeping an eye on him. But not a close enough one, by the sound of it.'

'Is he Caitlin's husband?' she asked.

'Ex,' he told her. 'They haven't lived together since the last time he was inside. But rumour has it that they're still seen in each other's company from time to time.'

'Yes, I saw them together a few days ago. But she wasn't with him on Friday.'

'I doubt if he'd try anything directly,' said Mitchell. 'Threats and low-level bullying are more in his line. But if he does much more of that he'll be in trouble anyway. Hmm. Maybe we should pull him in and have a word. We might find out more than we bargain for... But I shouldn't be worrying you with all this. Just steer clear of him, if you can.'

'I'll try,' said Pamela. 'I'd better warn Andy too.'

'Yes, do that.'

'Thank you,' she said. She opened the car door. 'I'll let you get on now. I'm sure you have more important things to do.'

He started the engine as she got out and closed the door. She thought he muttered something like 'never apologise' but she had turned away by then.

'Sorry,' said Andy when she went back into the house. 'I meant to ask about the wheelie-bin. Iris and Derek had theirs out last night.'

'They would!'

'Did you know there's a new word for people like them?'

'I can't imagine what it is,' she said, laughing. Should she really be encouraging him?

'Binfluencers. They're the first people to put out their bin, so everybody else just copies them.'

Pamela was grateful the new word had turned out to be less scurrilous than she had feared.

She was glad to have spoken to the detective inspector. Kim even called at lunchtime to find out what he'd said. Pamela kept it as vague as she could, and didn't mention the car incident. The last thing she wanted was for Kim to insist on moving in with her to ensure she was never alone. She was fond of her friend but had never had the slightest desire to live with her. They would have driven each other mad within the first twenty-four hours.

'You'll have to introduce me to him some time soon,' Kim said.

'I don't know if you'd get on,' said Pamela primly.

Kim just laughed and ended the call.

'Do you want me to walk the dogs today?' asked Andy half an hour or so later. 'It'll help to stop me getting nervous about the next exam.'

'I could do with the walk,' said Pamela. 'After all, we didn't get one yesterday after all… We can go to the woods. If we stick to the paths, surely I won't be silly enough to fall again.'

'I bet the detective inspector didn't think it was silly of you,' said Andy.

Pamela sighed. 'All right, he didn't. He's going to check it out. At this rate the police will have a huge file on me. They're probably even now discussing whether to arrest me for wasting so much of their time.'

They had a companionable walk in the woods, not saying very much but focussing on the dogs, who made the most of being let off their leads for a while. After Tiger showed signs of too much interest in what looked like either a very large rabbit-hole or a small badger sett, they clipped the leads back on and returned to the car.

If it hadn't been for all that had happened – and all that was still happening, apparently – Pamela would have enjoyed living on this side of town. It was a good place for the dogs and… She suddenly recalled that she hadn't even known about the dogs when she and Paul had decided to move here. Though Paul must have known, of course. Had he planned to dump them on her at some point, or was that an unfair assumption? More likely he'd chosen Cramond because of its convenience as far as his double life was concerned.

She tried to imagine what it might have been like if he'd still been alive, living with her in the bungalow at weekends and probably less than a mile away during the week. Surely it had been a high-risk strategy on his part. They could easily have bumped into each other somewhere nearby. It was almost as if he had wanted to be found out, to have the whole thing brought into the open – why? So that the two women could get together and solve the whole thing between them? So that she would understand he wanted to divorce her without him having to ask outright for it? Whatever he'd been thinking, it was quite wrong-headed.

Why hadn't she suspected something once she knew he'd only be home at weekends? It wasn't as if his work took him hundreds of miles away. Glasgow was easily within commuting distance. Lots of people went to and fro every day.

When she and Andy got home, she knew she had to escape somehow from the spiral of negative thoughts. It wouldn't do any good to blame Paul at this point, even if the whole mess was of his own making.

No, what she needed to do was to try and make sense of things, and to do that she had to sketch it all out.

She took out one of her largest pieces of paper and tilted the part of her desk that formed a drawing slope, then set to work.

In the centre she drew herself and Andy, and added the two dogs for good measure. Tiger and Lily had followed her into the studio, so she could draw them from life, which was fun. She and Andy were more stylised, almost caricatures.

She sketched Paul above and midway between herself and Andy, and then Joanne at Andy's side, then paused. A better methodology for the other characters in this drama might be to draw them on separate, smaller pieces of paper, or even on sticky-notes – though she hated sticky-notes – so that she could move them about if necessary. Yes, that was a good idea.

After about fifteen minutes, she had the people she considered to be the main players. Caitlin French, in her school crossing uniform complete with lollipop, her former partner, whose name she had forgotten, and his ugly dog. Then there was Eleanor Sharp, perhaps not a major character but somebody with a good deal of stage presence. Detective Chief Inspector Mitchell. Did she really need to include him? It was fun to sketch him anyway, particularly once she thought of adding a deerstalker and pipe. She considered adding a violin but that was overkill. She also debated with herself whether to add Iris and Derek, who, although extremely annoying, must surely only be innocent bystanders. They did have a boat, though. Hmm.

She sketched in a quick boat, and stuck the picture of Iris and Derek, an inseparable pair, next to it. Maybe the background should have been a map, but she'd have had to start again to make that work well. If there was a map, the boat could be placed conveniently at the mouth of the river Almond, and several of the characters would be walking along the promenade where she had met them. She wasn't very good at maps anyway, though it would have been nice to be able to illustrate the fact that Paul had moved studios and flats within Glasgow before his return to Edinburgh. The lawyers had never got back to her about the Glasgow flat, she realised. Unless she had missed a call from them, which she didn't think she had.

Then there were the jewels and the dog-napper and the intruder in her garden. She sketched in a heap of jewels in one corner of the large sheet.

The dog-napper and the man in the garden were faceless, in the sense that she hadn't seen their faces clearly enough to recognise them again – or at all, in the case of the man in the garden. In fact, she only knew about the intruder because Iris and Derek had told her about him. Pamela wondered if she could get a description of any kind out of them. The police would probably be interested in that too.

It might only have taken one person to damage her tyres and loosen the wheel-nuts. That might be where the intruder in the garden fitted in. She drew a dark faceless figure next to the car sketch she'd added almost without thinking about it.

Lauriston Castle had materialised at the far side of the page and gardens had sprung to life all round it by the time Andy came to find her and ask if she would mind if he cooked something for them, which of course she didn't mind at all. At first he stared in surprise at what she'd been doing, and then he leaned closer to view the detail.

'Is that us in the middle? Cool!'

'I'm just trying to make sense of the whole thing. I usually find I can do that once I visualise it – I'm having trouble with all this, though. There must be a missing link somewhere that we haven't seen.'

'An invisible link,' said Andy slowly. 'Apart from all the others, you mean?'

'Exactly,' said Pamela. 'An invisible missing link. That's all we need.'

A bit later, eating a passable lasagne, she reflected on this and wondered what the consequences of finding any more connections between some of the events might be. There was no knowing whether the next step might see herself and Andy being locked up, for all she knew.

Chapter 26 Worst Case

Pamela wished she hadn't even considered the possibility of one of them being locked up. She watched as Andy got into the police car at around lunchtime the following day and was driven off, and wondered if she should have protested or contacted a lawyer or anything. Maybe she should contact a lawyer now. She doubted if he had one he could call on. She would tell them to stand by, as it might look suspicious if they were too quick to intervene at this point. After all, the two police officers had just said they wanted to ask him a few more questions. They hadn't mentioned the word 'arrest', so for the moment at least she supposed he was going with them on a voluntary basis.

She sighed and turned to go back into the house.

There was no way she could get on with any work now, so she called the lawyers' office anyway. If nothing else, she wanted to ask if they'd had any luck with tracing Paul's property transactions under his other name. She supposed it didn't really matter at this point if he had swapped one studio for another, or one Glasgow flat for something similar, but she decided it was worthwhile collecting the information anyway. After all, if you were doing a jigsaw puzzle, you wanted all the pieces to be available, even if you couldn't see in the early stages where some of them fitted.

The woman she spoke to didn't know what she was talking about as far as the property search was concerned and said none of the people who might know were around. She did, on the other hand, know that they didn't usually handle criminal cases. She suggested a couple of legal firms who might be able to help.

Pamela ended the call with the feeling that her lawyers didn't want to get mixed up with anything as sordid as crime, although surely they must have been forced to do so at times. She couldn't face calling another firm of lawyers. Instead she would take the dogs out and hope the fresh air might clear her head.

In a kind of gesture of defiance, she took them round to Silverknowes promenade. She wasn't sure who the defiance was aimed at. Maybe the world in general. Anyway, she didn't plan to spend the rest of her life having her choices limited by people of dubious intent. Sooner or later she'd have to go where she liked and do what she chose to do. There had to be some advantages of widowhood, after all.

The day was grey and overcast, and Pamela found the sound of the descending planes more ominous than she ever had before. The fact that they tended to appear suddenly out of the looming cloud and always looked as if they were flying dangerously low didn't help either. On the plus side, there weren't as many walkers, cyclists or dogs there as usual. She wondered if it might be a matter of timing.

She walked down the slope and turned along the promenade past the café, going in the opposite direction from the posts marking the causeway, as was her preference.

When she turned the corner into the next bay and let the dogs off their leads, the first person she saw was Eleanor Sharp.

Pamela speeded her steps to catch up with the woman.

'I didn't think you were supposed to walk on your own any more,' said Eleanor.

'Didn't you?' said Pamela, trying to put on a wide-eyed innocent look although she knew it wouldn't suit her.

Eleanor laughed. 'Not according to Mal Mitchell, anyway. He seemed quite confident that you'd do as you were told, the last time I spoke to him. Still, at least we can walk this bit together.'

'But weren't you heading back the other way?'

'Yes, but Kenny can always manage to go a bit further. He's an easy-going creature.'

'What kind of dog is he?' said Pamela, conscious of her ignorance as she usually was when she spoke to Eleanor.

'Border terrier. They're the best dogs I've had. Resilient, patient and so on – most of the time, anyway. All dogs have their moments.' She turned to walk alongside Pamela. 'Couldn't you have brought the boy with you? Or is he doing something else?'

Pamela paused for a moment. She found herself reluctant to tell anybody else, even Eleanor, about Andy being taken away in the police car. Once she told somebody else, it would become more real, more serious.

'He's busy,' she said.

She half-expected Eleanor to say something about the devil finding work for idle hands, but the woman was oddly silent. They walked slowly along, Lily sticking closely to their heels while Kenny walked sedately alongside and Tiger darted to and fro in front of them.

'Have you heard from the police again?' asked Eleanor suddenly.

'Not really,' said Pamela. 'It's quite frustrating – I have no idea whether they're making any progress or not. I don't suppose they'd tell me, either way.'

'No,' Eleanor agreed. 'Even Mal Mitchell can be quite secretive. Do you want me to grill him for you?'

'No!' said Pamela. The word came out a little more fiercely than she intended. 'I mean – what if he thinks it's all my doing? You wouldn't be able to pass that on to me, would you? I might leave the country before he can catch me.'

Eleanor laughed. 'I think you're well into the realms of fantasy there.'

'Maybe,' said Pamela. 'I can't help wondering, though. You do hear of the wrong people being arrested.' Out of the corner of her eye she suddenly caught sight of two people apparently fighting, halfway up the nearby grass slope that rose up from the promenade. 'What's going on up there?'

'Probably just kids messing about,' said Eleanor after a cursory glance in the same direction. 'Do you want to turn back? If they come this way…'

'No, wait!' Pamela narrowed her eyes. It was hard to make out any detail at this range, and yet… 'One of them seems to be a girl – or a woman.'

Eleanor appeared doubtful. 'We still don't have to get involved. I suppose we could call the police if you think it's serious.'

Pamela thought about Mal Mitchell and an instinct that told her he wouldn't want any more work to land on his plate, and shook her head.

'You're probably right, it's just kids.'

She glanced back up at the figures on the slope. One of them broke away from the other and seemed to be trying to run away, only to be grabbed by the other and hauled back into the fray. Pamela realised that the reason she felt uneasy about them was that they somehow reminded her of Caitlin French and her ugly ex-husband, though if it was indeed him he didn't appear to have brought the even uglier dog along today. But if their relationship was all in the past, why would they have resorted to brawling in public like this?

Without another word Pamela handed her dogs' leads to Eleanor and set off up the slope at the nearest she could manage to a run. She had no idea where the urge to protect Caitlin had come from, though she told herself she would have done the same for any woman who seemed to be in trouble.

'Be careful!' Eleanor called after her. 'I'll have to call Mal Mitchell if you…'

The rest of the sentence was lost. Pamela, halfway towards the scene of the fight, could only hear the sound of her own breathing as it came harder and faster.

Somebody was shouting. She looked up. Caitlin's ex – Alan French – had seen her, and reacted with a stream of threats couched in the kind of language Pamela hadn't heard since she'd inadvertently caught a few minutes of a popular crime series on television. Did the police really talk like that amongst themselves?

She made herself ignore these stray thoughts and return to the moment. Alan French was now a bit too close for comfort.

'Just run!' cried Caitlin, who had somehow got hold of his arm and was trying vainly to hold him back. 'Your friend's waiting for you.'

Alan French turned and slapped his ex-wife across the face, so hard that she fell over backwards.

'I can't just go...' Pamela didn't even know where her thoughts were heading, never mind forming them into words.

'You heard her – get lost!' he said, this time in a low, dangerous tone that was more frightening than his previous tirade.

But he looked away suddenly and began to smile, which was even more sinister. Pamela followed the direction of his gaze. Another figure had emerged from the clump of trees at the top of the grassy slope, and was advancing on them. She blinked. It couldn't possibly be Iris from next-door, could it? What was she doing here at this precise moment?

Caitlin had struggled up to her hands and knees. 'No!' she cried. 'Don't!'

It wasn't clear who she was addressing. Pamela started towards her to try and help her to her feet, while Iris approached inexorably.

Pamela glanced back down to the promenade. Eleanor stood stock-still, the dogs arranged round her in a tableau that was only marred by Tiger, pulling at his lead and yapping, although Pamela could only hear the sound faintly.

'No! Leave me alone!' Caitlin snapped, pushing her away. 'Go back down to your friend. Please.'

At that moment Alan's arms clamped round Pamela's waist and he dragged her away from Caitlin. Pamela began to struggle.

'It's all right,' said Iris briskly, striding up to them. 'I can take it from here… Come on, Pamela, I'll give you a lift home. The car's just up there, behind the trees.'

'Thank you, but...'

Alan let her go suddenly and she stumbled a little. Iris grasped her by the arm, and she stared from woman to man in puzzlement. What possible connection could there be between the two of them? Unless Iris had just happened to be on her way down to the promenade, heard the noise and decided to intervene? That would fit with what Pamela already knew of the woman and her propensity to interfere, of course, but it was still extremely odd.

'Maybe you could take me back to my car,' she suggested. 'It's parked further along, near the café.'

Iris nodded without speaking, and tugged a little on her arm to start her moving. Well, that was all right. There couldn't be any harm in getting a lift back to the car, after all. It was no distance, and if she went off peaceably with Iris, Eleanor wouldn't feel the urge to run up the slope, encumbered by the three dogs, to rescue her from some imagined danger.

'Don't go!' cried Caitlin, but whatever else she'd intended to say was cut off abruptly.

Glancing back over her shoulder, Pamela saw that Alan had pulled his ex-wife to her feet but he'd placed his hand over her mouth to keep her quiet.

'Shouldn't we...?' Pamela began, but Iris interrupted in clipped tones.

'They've got to sort it out between themselves.'

Her grip tightened, and Pamela's unease deepened.

'I should really go back down for the dogs,' she said, gesturing down to the promenade, where Eleanor had now started moving again, presumably because Tiger had worked himself up into a frenzy. Maybe if she could just shrug off Iris's grip...

'Never mind the dogs!'

Iris glanced towards Eleanor and even gave her a little wave with her free hand.

'Calm down,' she added. 'We're nearly there.'

They'd reached the clump of trees. Soon they'd be out of Eleanor's sight. Pamela tried again to wrench her arm out of Iris's grip but if anything the woman only held on more tightly. Once they came out from the shelter of the trees, the road was in front of them, and a car neatly parked at the kerb.

'There,' said Iris. 'You see? It's no trouble to run you home.'

'No,' said Pamela. 'Back to my car. If you don't mind,' she added.

'If that's what you want, dear,' said Iris.

It wasn't really what Pamela wanted, but she didn't see that she had much choice in the matter.

Chapter 27 An Unexpected Journey

'Come along, hop in,' said Iris. 'It always seems longer on foot. All that walking you do with those dogs of yours – you need a bit of a rest from it.'

Pamela hesitated, reluctant to commit herself to getting into the car. It wasn't even facing the right way.

'But you'd have to turn round,' she said.

Iris laughed. 'I can do that. There's room to turn in the road just here, but if that bothers you we can go up to the roundabout and come back down the other way.'

Iris's laugh suddenly had a sinister tone in it. Don't be silly, Pamela told herself. You're going into the realms of fantasy again. Imagining Eleanor saying it in her no-nonsense voice emboldened her a little, and she scurried round the car and opened the passenger door to get in.

'Who's that woman the dogs are with?' enquired Iris as they went round the next corner and swooped up towards the roundabout.

'It's Eleanor. Eleanor Sharp, the vet.'

'Oh yes? I don't think I know her, but then we've never had any need for a vet. Not since our Katie left home, anyway. She did have a rabbit for a while.'

Katie. Iris had mentioned her once before. Pamela frowned. Why did the name suddenly ring alarm bells?

She was still puzzling over it when she realised Iris hadn't gone right round the roundabout and back the other way as she had said she would, but had turned right. They were heading along the short stretch of dual carriageway that Pamela knew led to another roundabout near the golf course.

'Sorry – I wanted to get back to my car,' she said.

Had Iris misunderstood her and thought she wanted to go straight home?

'Could you let me off as near the next roundabout as you can, please? I can walk back down to the car from there.'

'I don't think I can do that, Mrs Prendergast,' said Iris, accelerating.

'Does Katie still live somewhere near here?' Pamela asked on impulse.

Iris threw her a look that glittered dangerously. 'Why do you ask?'

'I just wondered,' said Pamela. She didn't particularly want to make Iris furious while driving, and it seemed she was in for a longer ride than she had expected.

They veered a little left at the next roundabout, went gradually uphill and came out on to a more major road just by the entrance to Lauriston Castle. Maybe Iris had misunderstood Pamela's request to go back to the car, and planned to take her home instead. Maybe the woman was a bit hard of hearing but not quite ready to admit it. Pamela's mother had taken ages to get round to wearing a hearing-aid, and even then she often forgot about it.

'It's fine if you just drop me at the house, then,' she said. Maybe she should resign herself to getting a taxi back to the place where she'd left the car. But Iris drove past the turning that would have taken them both to their respective bungalows, and went on until they reached the way down to Cramond village, with its historic church, partly excavated Roman fort and picturesque old houses. And the causeway to the island.

'Are you going to pick up Derek?' Pamela asked.

'Derek? Why should I pick him up?'

'I thought maybe he was down at the harbour on your boat or something.'

'No, he's at home... He gets out less and less. I suppose I might have to start looking at care homes if he goes downhill any further.'

'Care homes?'

'Well, he won't be able to be of any more use to me in the house or on the boat, if his dementia gets any worse,' said Iris.

Won't be of any more use? Pamela shivered.

'Are you cold?' Iris frowned. 'Well, there's no point in turning the heater up now that we're nearly there. You should have said something earlier... Have you got any experience of handling a boat?'

'No,' said Pamela. 'Sorry.'

'Pity,' said Iris. 'You could have given me a hand with the ropes – on the way out anyway. Still, I've sailed on my own before.'

'Um – where are we going?'

'Never you mind that,' said Iris. 'You'll find out soon enough.'

Iris made a tricky turn with ease and proceeded along the road next to the harbour. She parked near a large building, the Boat Club headquarters. It seemed as if this was a quiet time. Pamela couldn't see anybody she thought she might be able to ask for help. A couple of very old men came along, but they both leaned heavily on walking-sticks, and she couldn't bring herself to involve them. Maybe the best thing was to try and keep Iris talking in a relatively calm way until – until what? How was it destined to end?

She shivered again as they got out of the car.

'Here we are,' said Iris, gesturing towards the river. 'We'll have to row out, of course. Are you any good at rowing?'

'I've done it a couple of times,' said Pamela cautiously. In truth she hadn't even set foot in a small boat since she was in her late teens and had gone out on a boating lake with Kim. Even then she hadn't been very handy with the oars. She wished fervently that she had Kim at her side now.

'Once we're on board we can get ourselves a cup of tea and wait for the tide,' said Iris, as if Pamela should know what she was talking about and why they were there. 'Here - the dinghy's at the bottom of the steps.'

They went down a flight of stone steps set into the harbour wall, and Iris helped Pamela into the small rowing-boat that waited there. It rocked alarmingly as they got in. Maybe if it capsized here, in the harbour, somebody would hear the sound and come to the rescue. Pamela decided not to risk making any sudden movements. Even in April being submerged in river water probably wouldn't be at all pleasant.

Iris seemed to have given up on expecting Pamela to row, and took the oars herself, managing them with brisk, practised movements. Within minutes they were bumping gently up against the side of one of the yachts moored in the river channel. Somehow or other she clambered up the rope ladder to reach the deck. She thought Iris, who was evidently stronger than she looked, must have propelled her from behind for most of the way, but her brain was working sluggishly and she was starting to wonder if this was all really happening.

There was a small cabin with bench seats, a table that seemed to be built in, and a two-ring gas hob. In an incongruous echo of that awkward tea-party in her house, Iris put the kettle on, brought out tea-cups decorated with tiny flowers, and began to take biscuits out of a tin and arrange them on a plate. It was warm inside the cabin and Pamela wriggled out of her jacket.

Iris glanced at her watch. 'We've got about half an hour yet to wait for the tide,' she said.

'Wait for the tide?' said Pamela, trying to kick-start her brain.

Iris gave her a scornful look. 'You'll have seen the mudflats. There's only a narrow channel across them, and it's only safe to sail out for a few hours a day. I checked today's times on my phone while I was waiting for you.'

Pamela desperately wanted to question this last statement, but she restrained herself. She didn't know if she even wanted to know why Iris had been waiting for her, or how she had managed to be in just the right place at the right time to catch her....

Had Caitlin had something to do with it? She frowned, remembering the younger woman's plea to her to go back down to Eleanor, and her last words as Pamela walked off with Iris – 'Don't go.' It was almost as if she knew, or suspected, what Iris planned to do, and hoped to avert it. Only her ex had prevented her from doing anything more useful.

What could Caitlin and Iris possibly have in common? How had they even met? Neither had even mentioned the other, unless...

'Our Katie's not interested at all.'

Pamela suddenly heard Derek's voice in her head. Katie! Could it be a short form of Caitlin?

Iris handed her a tea-cup complete with matching saucer, interrupting her unsettling thought processes.

'There we are – you'll be glad of a hot drink inside you when we get out into the Forth.'

'I just hope it'll stay inside me,' murmured Pamela, accepting the drink.

She took a small sip of the tea.

'Oh, did you want sugar?' said Iris, sitting down on the opposite bench with her cup. 'Would you like a biscuit with it?'

'No sugar, thanks,' said Pamela. 'I'd better not have a biscuit either – I'm trying to cut down.'

She wasn't actually averse to a biscuit or two, or even three if the occasion demanded it, but her new-found suspicions caused her to be a little reluctant to accept any food or drink at Iris's hands. What on earth could she do about the tea? She glanced about her to see if there were any possible receptacles into which she could easily pour it without being too obvious.

'Drink up, then,' said Iris. 'Or would you have preferred coffee? Sorry, I forgot to ask. I'm not sure if we have any on board anyway. Derek always likes a cup of tea before sailing, so I've got used to that over the years… All those years… He didn't even ask how we paid for the boat, or the bungalow. Anything. He was always content to accept whatever I gave him. Don't you think that's how marriages should work, Mrs Prendergast? Or were you and Paul different from the rest of us?'

Her tone was disparaging, as if she knew exactly how her marriage had operated, and didn't think much of it.

'I suppose everybody finds their own way,' said Pamela mildly.

She took another tiny sip of the tea, deliberately spilling some of it in the saucer as she put the cup down again. Iris wasn't looking in this direction, so with luck she hadn't noticed anything. But the saucer was bound to overflow before long. She must find another way.

'I wouldn't have known, you know,' said Iris. 'About his double life, I mean. I only knew him as Paul Hutchison, Joanne's husband. Just imagine my surprise when I found he had a driving licence in his pocket in the name of Paul Prendergast. And a wedding photo in his wallet, only the woman in the photo wasn't Joanne. It was you, wasn't it? A good bit younger then, though.'

She gave an unpleasant laugh.

Pamela recalled finding the wedding photo in the box from Paul's studio. In spite of everything, it seemed he had still carried a smaller copy of it about with him. When he was in character as Paul Prendergast, that was. Presumably he had a whole different set of belongings for when he was Paul Hutchison. She thought again about all the trouble he had gone to. Had it ever been worth it?

'Then you moved in next to us,' Iris continued. 'That was another surprise, but at least it gave me the chance to find out how much of a risk you were to us. I wasn't sure until the boy moved in. After that it was only a matter of time.'

She glanced at her watch. Pamela considered the possibility that time might stand still and giving her a reprieve.

There was a shout from outside, and Iris stood up and went out on the deck. Pamela listened with half an ear, in the act of pouring most of the rest of her tea on to the floorboards under her feet. She shuffled her feet about in the liquid, hoping it would move into a less obvious place. She had no idea, of course, whether there had been anything wrong with the drink and even if there was, she didn't know what kind of effect it was expected to produce. Should she pretend drowsiness, or even something more dramatic. She doubted if Iris had access to anything more lethal than sleeping-pills, although if she did indeed have criminal connections maybe it was something worse than that.

The most likely option, she calculated, was that she was meant to be too sleepy to resist when Iris took the next step, which, it was not such a wild guess, would have something to do with sailing out into the Forth.

Iris returned to the cabin.

'Well, that was a waste of time,' she said. 'Just some old man warning me not to take the boat out until the tide was right. As if I didn't know that! I said to him, if I'd needed advice from an old man I'd have brought my own with me.' She laughed. 'He didn't know what to say to me after that… Are you all right, Mrs Prendergast?'

For Pamela had decided to go for the simplest option, and she'd closed her eyes and slumped a little to one side.

She opened her eyes quickly. 'I'm fine,' she said. 'Absolutely fine. Never felt…'

She let her voice trail away into silence.

'Good,' said Iris. 'I'm glad to hear it… We should be getting ready to go soon. Just you stay there and feel fine and I'll get everything sorted.'

Iris moved about outside the cabin, and even hummed a tune now and then. With luck, Pamela thought, she hadn't overdone the drowsiness. She had always avoided any kind of acting, whether on or off the stage. It was a little intimidating to have to make her debut under these circumstances, when she hadn't seen the script and didn't know what part she was supposed to be playing.

She wondered if this was what had happened to Paul. Was she to meet just the same fate as he had, or would she simply be taken out to deeper water and thrown overboard? Pamela made up her mind in that moment that she wasn't going to meet that fate, no matter what she had to do to avoid it.

Chapter 28 Marooned

'Don't go right off.' Iris was shaking her by the shoulder. 'I need you to come on deck.'

'Mmm,' said Pamela, without opening her eyes.

The boat was rocking a little, maybe in anticipation of sailing out on the tide.

Iris slapped her face lightly. 'Come on. Let's go now. The fresh air should bring you round a bit, and we need to leave in a minute or there won't be time.'

Pamela let her eyes flutter open. 'Mmm? My jacket?'

The other woman smiled. 'You won't need that where you're going.'

She let herself stumble out on the deck, opening one eye to make sure she didn't stumble over the side, though she guessed Iris wouldn't let her do so while they were still in the harbour. Wouldn't it be better to do just that? It would be amusing to see Iris's reaction if she did it, and it would certainly have been less foolhardy than what she actually intended to do, which was to wait until Iris reached the point of incriminating herself – which, if all went according to plan, she would feel compelled to do, as with any good tv villain - and then take the woman by surprise and overpower her. Pamela could only imagine how Eleanor Sharp, Detective Chief Inspector Mitchell, Andy, Kim, almost anybody she knew, would react. If they ever found out, that was. On a more sober note, it was perfectly possible that they would never know.

But those were defeatist thoughts. In a way she supposed she planned to avenge Paul, while in another way she just wanted the nightmare to end, one way or the other. She certainly couldn't carry on indefinitely like this, unable to go where she wanted, fearful and anxious, unable to do her work because of intrusive thoughts about Paul's death, their failed marriage that had seemed so functional and sensible at the time, and the other life he had led.

At last it seemed to be time to leave the mooring and head out into the channel. Iris bustled about the deck, doing things with ropes, and then settled at the wheel, which Pamela hadn't even noticed at first. The engine came to life. At least there was no hoisting of sails to delay them even further. The start of the endgame. Or the end of the beginning, or whatever.

Iris concentrated on the steering for a while as they made their way into the Forth, passing the causeway on their right and seeing the island looming up before them, larger and more forbidding against a pewter sky. Had there been bad weather forecast? Pamela usually only listened to the forecast with half an ear, feeling she didn't need to worry about it one way or the other. It was different for sailors, of course. Iris probably had it all memorised.

They altered course slightly to veer round to the far side of the island. They weren't far off the shore at this point. Were they going right round to the other side of the causeway?

Pamela closed her eyes again, clinging to the rail at the edge of the deck. The waves were rougher here. Was she going to be sick?

Stop worrying about that. Think about what to do. If they went any further out, she would have no chance of swimming ashore. What if she went over the side now, and swam to the island? Was there anywhere to make landfall, or would she end up clinging to slippery rocks and unable to clamber up?

She reached down and slipped her shoes off. That would make swimming for it a little easier.

'Ah,' said Iris. 'I see you've caught on at last. It took you a while, didn't it? Not as clever as you thought you were?'

The woman was coming towards her now, brandishing some kind of nautical tool. It looked rather heavy, as if it could do some damage.

Pamela picked up one of her shoes and threw it. She didn't wait to see if it had made contact, but ducked under the rail and slid feet first into the water. She felt something hit her shoulder as she went.

The water was icy cold, and at first she couldn't work out which way the current was taking her – if it carried her out into the middle of the Forth she guessed she'd have little or no chance of survival.

Her shoulder hurt so she turned on to her back and kicked her feet up. That was better. She gritted her teeth and continued, not knowing where she was going, but still able to see the boat as she put some distance between herself and it. Then it changed direction and began to move slowly closer after all.

It was almost on her again when her head bumped into something. A rock. She turned and grabbed hold of it, and saw at the same time that it wasn't part of a rocky outcrop but just one rock standing up at the edge of a pebble beach. She dragged herself out of the water and collapsed on the pebbles. She couldn't stay there for long. Iris might be able to beach the boat just as Pamela had beached herself.

But then she heard a thud followed by an ominous creaking and groaning sound, and turned her head to look for the boat. Iris hadn't been able to beach it after all. Instead she must have run into a cluster of rocks not far out from the shore, and as Pamela watched, she saw that the boat was lurching to one side, with Iris clinging to a rail. Presumably she'd been so focussed on pursuing Pamela that she hadn't taken enough notice of where she was, or whatever charts she used to navigate.

'Call the lifeboat,' Pamela muttered, giving herself instructions.

She felt for her phone, but of course she'd taken off her jacket while still on the boat and the phone was in the pocket. What could she do? She couldn't just watch while Iris went down with her ship – or could she?

The only sensible thing she could think of to do was to try to make it across the island to the causeway in the faint hope that the tide hadn't covered it more than ankle-deep by this time – which must be a very long shot if Iris had waited for enough coverage to bring the boat out without getting stuck on the way.

Even once she was on the causeway, she thought wildly, it would take her a while to cross it, even longer if she had to wade through waist-deep water. Was that even feasible? She remembered seeing newspaper reports of the lifeboat having to rescue people who had attempted to cross at the wrong times. She had thought how silly and reckless they were.

What else could she do? She knew without even considering it very carefully that she didn't have the strength to do anything about saving the boat. Or even Iris, who would likely try to drag her into the water, or hit her again with the implement she'd used the last time. Pamela's shoulder gave a twinge as she remembered it. The other woman would just have to survive until help arrived, so the sooner that happened the better. She guessed Iris's chances of survival were somewhat greater than her own, in any case. The woman was strong, and knew her way around boats. She might even be able to put out a distress signal of some kind.

Getting to the causeway was still the best option for both of them, she told herself firmly, trying to quell the urge to turn back. Maybe she could find a way of alerting somebody on the mainland from there. She couldn't very well light a fire – she guessed it would take her all night to ignite it by rubbing sticks together or whatever Scouts and Guides used to do. But maybe waving something…

First reach the causeway, she told herself, then think about the next step.

With one backward glance at the boat, with Iris still in sight and clinging on, Pamela set off. She made heavy weather of the pebble beach, but once she had clambered up on to the grass behind it the going was a little easier. The sky was darkening, so rain must be on the way. Still, she probably couldn't get any wetter than she already was.

She found a narrow path, the kind that sheep might use, except that there weren't any sheep. It led her into the interior of the island, where there was a wooded area. Brambles and nettles reached out to grab at her legs from both sides of the path, but she pushed on regardless. She couldn't feel anything much below her knees anyway. That was another advantage of being wet through and chilled. But as long as she kept moving, she'd probably be all right.

Fuelled by optimism, she followed the path into the cover of the trees and almost immediately bumped into somebody coming the other way.

They both stepped back abruptly.

'Sorry!' she said. 'I didn't know there was anybody else here.'

'Have you been swimming or something?' said the young woman, regarding her critically. 'Wasn't it a bit cold?'

'I need to call the police, and the lifeboats,' said Pamela. 'There's been an accident – a boat. On the rocks.'

A young man emerged from the tent that she now saw was partly concealed among the trees.

'No police,' he said firmly. 'Maybe we can help with the boat.'

'I need the police for something else too,' said Pamela. 'Have you got a phone?'

'You should try and get warm first,' the young woman advised. 'We've got sleeping-bags. Here, get in the tent.'

'I've got to do something about the boat,' Pamela insisted. 'If you won't help, I'll have to go to the causeway and try to cross.'

'Can't be done,' said the young man. 'Tide's in.'

'How far in? Can I still wade across?'

'No way,' said the young man.

'Have you got matches or anything, then?' said Pamela. 'I need to send a signal.'

The two young people looked at each other, and the young woman sighed.

'It's a dare,' she said. 'We've got to spend the night here. If the police start trampling all over the place, they'll make us leave.'

'I won't tell them about you,' said Pamela.

'They'll know, if we call them from our phone... We've got a lantern. Maybe you can use that to send a signal? You could say you found it somewhere. People are always leaving things lying about here. We found somebody's backpack under a bush.'

'We still can't risk the police coming,' said the young man. 'We'll get into trouble.'

'But not if it was to save somebody's life,' said Pamela. 'You'd be heroes.'

She had to suppress the urge to snap at them. There wasn't time for all this, but she could tell they'd probably just dig their heels in even further if she pushed too much for what she wanted.

She couldn't suppress a shiver, however. Now that she had stopped moving, she felt the cold right through to her bones.

'Can I use your lantern to signal, then?' she asked. 'You've got time to hide somewhere – what about those old buildings? Look – there's a wall just up there. You could move your tent behind it. The police wouldn't be bothered about you. It'll be nearly dark by the time they get here anyway.'

'Maybe we should let her do it,' said the young woman uncertainly, glancing at the man for confirmation.

'All right,' he said reluctantly. 'But you have to leave the lantern in a safe place after you've finished with it. We need it for tonight.'

'It's a deal,' said Pamela.

They showed her how to switch the lantern on and off, and insisted on accompanying her to a rise in the ground from which they could see the causeway and the little beach alongside the start of it.

'Leave it in the rocks there. We'll be gone as soon as you start.'

Pamela tried to force her half-frozen brain to remember Morse Code or any signal she might possibly make using a lantern that only seemed to have on and off settings and none of the fancier functions. In the end she settled for a series of flashes. Was the beam powerful enough to reach some casual watcher on the mainland? She didn't know, and almost didn't care at this point. At least she was doing something about the situation.

After a while the lantern seemed dimmer than before and eventually it wasn't producing any light at all. She hoped the two of them wouldn't be angry that she'd run the batteries right down. Maybe they would have some way of re-charging it. She wedged it into the rocks in the place they'd shown her, and went and leaned against the wall of one of the buildings – a war-time installation, by the look of it – to wait and see if there was any response to her signalling attempts.

She heard a buzzing noise – was it in her own ears or was it in the sky, or on the water? It nagged at the edge of her consciousness for a while and then stopped.

Despite the chill that now seemed as if it had taken up permanent residence inside her, she found her eyes closing once the sky darkened further and there was only grey twilight wherever she looked.

Chapter 29 From Twilight to Morning

Pamela knew it would be dangerous to fall asleep. She might never wake up.

With her last vestiges of strength, she pushed herself to her feet, unsure of whether she could even trust her legs to hold her upright. At that moment, as she looked towards the mainland, she saw flashing blue lights, and figures hurrying about, and then, hugging the line of the pillars that marked the route of the causeway, a small boat heading her way.

She waved her arms to try and attract attention, then, moving very cautiously because she still wasn't entirely certain her legs were working, she felt her way down over the rocks to the sandy beach below, and waited there.

Should she wave again, or shout this time? Maybe they hadn't seen her.

But there were people talking not very far away, presumably in the little boat, and a few moments later somebody approached out of the dimness.

'Aha!' he said when he was closer. 'I might have known – Pamela Prendergast.'

Of course it had to be Detective Chief Inspector Mitchell, of all people.

'The boat,' she said. 'You've got to rescue Iris. It's round at the far side of the island. Stuck on the rocks.'

'Don't you worry about the boat,' he told her. 'Or about Iris. They reached her a wee while ago. That's how we knew about you.'

It didn't make any sense, but she didn't have the energy to think it through.

A second officer came up to them, armed with a foil blanket to wrap round her.

'But Iris,' Pamela began.

'There's been a helicopter on the scene already,' Mitchell told her. 'And the lifeboat. They heard about the wreck from a pilot who happened to be passing.'

'Happened to be passing?'

'Overhead. In the sky,' he said. 'Just turned to fly up river to the airport. He saw the wreck and radioed in.'

She remembered the planes she'd seen on their descent to the airport, flying almost directly above her head, getting lower and lower and then disappearing, shielded from view by the trees.

'Oh, yes!' she exclaimed. 'I hadn't thought of that.'

'Then there was the call from Mrs French too. She insisted on coming down to the harbour – wants to speak to you, but we can hurry you past her if you want.'

'Mrs French? Caitlin?'

'That's her,' said Mitchell. 'She let us know you'd gone off with Iris, so we were hoping the lifeboat people would find you on the boat. She'll be happy to know you didn't go overboard.'

'I did, actually,' said Pamela. 'But of my own volition, not because anybody pushed me. I swam to the beach. Is Iris all right? I didn't want to leave her on her own.'

'As far as we know, yes. Come on, let's get you home now. We can talk about it later… Eleanor says not to worry about the dogs. She's waiting with them and the boy at yours, with hot drinks and whatever. We just need to check in with the paramedics first.'

'Paramedics?'

'You wouldn't want them to have a wasted journey, now would you?'

'But how did you…?'

Halfway through the sentence, Pamela realised she was too tired to finish it. She allowed herself to be shepherded on to the little boat, ferried ashore and given the all-clear by the paramedics. They let Caitlin French have a quick word with her and then for some reason both she and Caitlin were in Mal Mitchell's car, being driven home. Eleanor and Andy gave her a warm welcome there, and the dogs an ecstatic one, and before long she was tucked up in bed, blanket round her shoulders, sipping hot chocolate. Lily lay alongside her and Tiger was by her feet, although she suspected he would retreat from that position as soon as she moved.

She hadn't thought she could possibly sleep that night, but at some point the images of the events of the day paused in their whirling progress round her mind and she didn't know anything more until something licked her face and she opened her eyes to see daylight in the gap at the side of the bedroom curtains.

Lily was the one who had made the fuss, of course, but Tiger was back on the bed too, though poised to jump off.

When she wriggled up to a sitting position her shoulder gave a twinge and the morning-after sting of bramble scratches around her ankles reminded her of her panicky dash across Cramond Island.

There was a brisk knock at the bedroom door, and it opened a little way. Eleanor's head appeared in the gap.

'Are you fit to get up for breakfast, or can we bring it in here?'

'I'll get up.'

Pamela hated breakfast in bed, and she knew it would be even worse with two dogs around to steal her toast.

'Coffee or tea?' said Eleanor.

'Oh, coffee please. Is Andy there? Is Caitlin still around?'

'Andy's here – Caitlin felt she had to go next-door and break the news to her father. She seems to think he won't manage well on his own, but that's not our problem. Andy and I are waiting to hear the whole story. But no pressure.'

Pamela laughed. 'I'll be ready in five minutes.'

As well as listening to her side of the story, they had their own tale to tell. After seeing Pamela vanish into the trees with Iris, Eleanor, despite being hampered by the three dogs, had set off up the slope towards Caitlin and Alan French. At the same time Alan had been dragging his ex-wife away in the direction of another wooded area.

'I couldn't decide what to do at that stage,' Eleanor confessed. 'Whether to call the police right away and wait for them, or to chase the two of them into the woods. I thought the dogs might get on their scent or something if I took them into the woods. It was silly of me. A waste of time.'

'You weren't to know,' said Pamela, so grateful to be safely in her own home eating toast and marmalade and listening to Eleanor's account as if it were only a story and not something they had all been part of, that she couldn't bring herself to feel aggrieved.

Eleanor shook her head. 'You know, whenever I saw women in tv thrillers putting themselves in danger, I always thought I was a sensible person who'd leave things up to the police. I used to shout at them sometimes not to do it. Not to set foot in the derelict building at night without telling anybody where you were going… But then, you probably thought the same. While you're actually living through it, you just keep going on autopilot until you run into the buffers.'

Pamela thought she understood Eleanor's point, despite the mixed metaphors. At the point when she first got into Iris's car, she had certainly not anticipated having to swim for her life.

'Anyway, after we'd searched the woods,' Eleanor continued, 'I went back down on to the promenade, and walked back towards the café. I didn't see any sign of you and Iris, or of Caitlin and Alan. I waited in the car for a bit and then drove along Marine Drive quite slowly, but I didn't see Caitlin until I was right up at the roundabout. I stopped for her, but it took me a while to persuade her to get in and tell me what was going on. She was in such a state by then that I could only make out about half of what she tried to tell me… But from what she did manage to communicate, I knew I had to call the police right away.'

'Iris and I must have been on board the boat by then,' said Pamela. 'Waiting for the tide to come in. She tried to drug me, but luckily I don't like tea at the best of times,' she added.

'We didn't know where she'd taken you. I came here in case she'd been trying to be helpful and brought you home. But she hadn't. The police hadn't found any sign of her car either. It wasn't until Andy got back and told us about the boat that things started moving.'

'She parked outside the boating club,' murmured Pamela. She glanced at Andy.

'I remembered looking at the boats with you that day, and I told the police what you'd said about Iris and Derek having one,' he said. 'I'd been wondering about Iris. She was too friendly.'

Eleanor and Pamela exchanged an amused glance.

'No,' said Andy, 'I mean the friendliness didn't seem real. I didn't like the way she barged into your house that day. And I saw her giving me funny looks too.'

'Is Iris all right?' said Pamela, suddenly remembering the last time she'd seen the woman.

'They've taken her to hospital,' said Eleanor with a dismissive shrug. 'She's still alive anyway. For what it's worth.'

'I don't know what possessed me to go aboard the boat with her,' said Pamela.

'I don't suppose you thought she was a serious threat,' said Eleanor. 'Not when you first got into the car anyway. That was your only mistake. I mean, thinking Caitlin was more of a danger than Iris was.'

'I didn't know Iris was a danger to me at all,' said Pamela. 'But she killed Paul, you know.'

She hadn't meant to come out with it quite so abruptly. She saw Andy flinch at her words. Eleanor, of course, took them in her stride.

'Mal Mitchell will be able to tell us more about that,' she said. 'He said he might drop round later, when he's got a minute.'

Drop round? The wording was a bit too casual for Pamela's liking. The police hadn't even had a proper account from her of what had happened on the boat. If she had felt stronger, she would have been tempted to find the nearest police officer and insist that he should take a statement from her.

As it happened, that wasn't necessary. Mal Mitchell's idea of dropping round turned out to mean he called first and arranged an appointment, and brought another police officer with him to interview her. He wasn't giving a lot away about his thoughts or about what had happened to Iris and to the boat, though he did tell her the lifeboat crew had found her jacket on board with the phone in the pocket, which was what had told the police she was somewhere about the island. They'd been preparing to mount a full-scale search there when somebody had seen her lantern signals.

'Handy, finding the lantern,' remarked the Chief Inspector. 'Still, it's amazing what some people leave lying about and forget.'

'Yes,' said Pamela.

He probably knew about the illicit campers, but maybe they were such small fry in the scheme of things that he wasn't too bothered about catching up with them.

'I'll have more to tell you later on,' he said. 'But don't hold your breath – we've got a lot of tidying up to do.'

Eleanor laughed when Pamela told her how Mitchell had phrased it.

'I just hope there aren't any dark dusty wee corners left over when they've finished,' she said. 'You never know when there might be scary spiders lurking somewhere.'

Pamela shuddered. 'I'd prefer not to think about spiders, if you don't mind.'

Chapter 30 Decluttered

Mal Mitchell was coming to tea. To celebrate, Pamela and Andy unpacked the last of the boxes so that there would be enough space for Andy to sleep, study and sculpt. He'd be going back to Mrs Paton's until the end of the college term, but Pamela suggested he might need somewhere as a home base, and he'd agreed. He had explained, rather earnestly, that he couldn't make full-size sculptures in his room but he could draw the designs, and occasionally make maquettes if he had only a little more space available.

'Maybe we should build a studio in the garden for you,' she told him, only half-joking.

'You need a studio more than me,' he said. 'I don't even know if I'll get anywhere with my sculpture. You're already making money out of your illustrations.'

'Money isn't the only thing to consider.'

He gave her a pitying look. 'You're only saying that because you've always had enough of it.'

She had already gathered from his stray remarks that money had been tight for the Hutchison family over the past couple of years. Paul must have been deluded to think he could run afford two households, particularly after Joanne had persuaded him to try and give up on the criminal connections which had eventually got them both killed.

But she would have to wait for the chief inspector to tell them the whole story. Or at least she hoped that was what would happen.

Eleanor had also invited herself round that afternoon. According to her, it was best to have an independent referee present on these occasions. Pamela wondered whether the vet had a lot of experience of similar situations. Had there even been any similar situations? There were so many ingredients in this one – bigamy, murder, jewel theft, gang warfare… the whole works really.

Still, it would be nice to have it all explained.

'It started a good few years ago, when your late husband was approached by a group of men who were involved in large-scale jewel theft. They'd found it next to impossible to get rid of all the proceeds of their robberies, because the most valuable items were much too easily recognised, so they needed an accomplice who could melt things down and put the gems into new settings. You'd think they would have sussed that side of it out before going into that line of business in the first place, but in our experience you get a lot of criminals who aren't capable of looking that far ahead.'

'I suppose that's why they make mistakes,' commented Pamela.

'If we're lucky, they make mistakes… Anyway, it seems that they made Mr Prendergast an offer he couldn't refuse, and he took the line of least resistance and agreed to do some work for them. Once he had a bit of extra money, he got used to it, and did a bit more of that kind of work on the side… As far as we can make out, he set up his second identity all those years ago to protect you, Mrs Prendergast.'

'To protect me?'

Pamela could scarcely believe Paul had ever thought that leading a double life would protect her from anything. It hadn't protected her from having to identify his body, or from being harassed by the people who wanted something from her after his death.

'He'd given those criminals a false name – Hutchison – and hadn't told them anything about his Edinburgh address. As far as they were concerned, he lived full-time in his flat in Glasgow. But once he'd gone down that road, things got more complicated. He got together with Joanne, who took on his name, either because they went through a fake marriage ceremony or just informally, and after a while they had Andy to think about too.'

Pamela shook her head. 'I don't know why he didn't just ask me for a divorce. We lived almost separately – it should have been an easy thing to do.'

'I suppose he didn't want to upset you,' said Mitchell.

'Funny way to go about it,' muttered Eleanor. 'Typical man.'

From wanting to scream and shout, Pamela suddenly found herself suppressing a laugh at this. She saw Mitchell glowering at both of them, but he continued his account.

'They moved out of Glasgow eventually, to try and get away – we think he'd decided to go straight at that stage.'

'Not before time,' said Pamela.

'Then it all went pear-shaped,' Mitchell continued. 'Some of the gang members tracked them down to the Silverknowes area, and from then on their lives weren't worth anything… Sorry, Andy… But I suppose you're all wondering how Iris and Caitlin come into the picture.'

'Yes,' said Pamela. 'I am.'

'Iris's husband Derek was one of the senior members of the gang of jewel thieves, before he went downhill that is. We've tried to talk to him but he doesn't seem able to function at all without Iris. Maybe she was the brains behind him all along, only the rest of them wouldn't want a woman ordering them around.... Caitlin was their daughter, and unfortunately she married into the family business, so to speak.'

'Katie,' said Pamela. 'I should have known the first time Iris mentioned her. Though I suppose I must just have assumed the daughter's real name was Katherine.'

'You weren't to know,' said Mitchell. 'Well, Iris and Derek more or less retired to Cramond – Iris had to get Derek out of harm's way, before he made too many mistakes or spoke to the wrong people – but the others in the gang called on them for assistance in silencing Mr Prendergast and Mrs Hutchison.'

'Mum and Dad,' murmured Andy.

Pamela had almost forgotten he was there. He sat in the corner, hugging Lily close to him, Tiger sitting on his feet. She was glad he had the two dogs for comfort. Should she have shut him out of this session? Or was it better that he knew the whole truth so that there were no more secrets?

Mitchell glanced over at Andy. 'I'm afraid their deaths were deliberate, son.'

'I thought so,' said Andy stoically.

'As you probably already know, Mrs Prendergast,' continued the detective inspector, 'Iris somehow talked your husband on to the boat – maybe in much the same way she got you there, just by refusing to listen to any protests. Then she would have drugged him, as she attempted to do in your case. She isn't talking yet, but from the photographs the technicians took we think it's possible she secured him to one of the concrete posts with a rope but got rid of it afterwards. Or maybe the force of the waves pulled it loose. It was a rough night. We may find out more yet.'

'He didn't deserve that,' said Pamela. 'No matter what he'd done.'

Andy gave her a faint smile.

'The fake accident on the pedestrian crossing was a bit harder to organise,' said Mitchell. 'There were several steps to it. Stealing Andy's phone so that somebody could call his Mum and talk her into crossing the road at just the right time. Caitlin was there, of course, and I suppose if it came to the crunch they might have tried to put the blame on her. She would have been well placed to push Mrs Hutchison into the path of the car if there was some problem with the timings. We've checked with other witnesses and there was no need for her still to be hanging around. All the kids were on their way by the time of the accident, but we spoke to a few older people she always used to help across the road... Anyway, her ex-husband and two of his brothers are in it up to their necks. They're the ones who've been causing trouble for Andy at various locations about here. It would have helped if we'd known about some of those incidents earlier, mind,' he added.

'What about the intruder in my garden?' said Pamela, determined to get as many answers as she could out of him while he was in this talkative mood.

'We think Iris and Derek invented him,' said Mitchell. 'Iris had the key to the house so she could come in any time and search for whatever they thought they were looking for. But she wanted to set up another suspect for that, in case you got suspicious.'

'The gemstones?' enquired Andy.

Mitchell nodded. 'We think that's what they were after. Incidentally, you'll be sorry to hear the ones you handed over to us earlier were all fakes. It seems as if Iris and maybe other members of the gang thought you had real ones stashed away somewhere, but it's also possible Mr Prendergast didn't have them any more, or had somehow cashed them in before his death.'

'Good,' said Pamela. 'I don't want anything to do with jewels, whether they're fake or real, or criminal gangs or murders or boats, ever again.'

''That makes sense,' said Mal Mitchell. 'Just you try and stick to it, and you won't go far wrong. I certainly don't want to have any more to do with you.... In a professional sense, I mean,' he added hastily.

Eleanor and Andy were glaring at him in unison. He must have felt he had to backtrack a little. And after all, Pamela told herself, they were sure to see each other in the garden from time to time. She pictured herself giving him a wave over the fence as she planted up the herbaceous border, or pruned the roses, or did whatever real gardeners did.

He would straighten from contemplating his prize marrows and wave back. It would all be perfectly civilised and amicable, without even a hint of crime to intrude on their respective garden idylls.

THE END

About the Author

Cecilia Peartree is the pen-name of a writer who lives in Edinburgh. She has been writing stories since she was 6 years old, and started to publish her work when she was somewhat older.
Many of her novels are contemporary mysteries, including the 25-book (so far) Pitkirtly Mysteries series and the shorter Max Falconer series. She has also written various novels set in the past, including the Adventurous Quest series of 1950s thrillers, and a handful of novels set in the Regency era. All her novels are currently available from Amazon as ebooks and most also as paperbacks.

Further information about all Cecilia's published novels as well as progress on new projects may be found on her website at https://ceciliapeartree.com.

Printed in Great Britain
by Amazon